This Dagger, My Heart

SUNY series in Contemporary Continental Philosophy

Dennis J. Schmidt, editor

This Dagger, My Heart

A Novel

DAVID FARRELL KRELL

SUNY
PRESS

Published by State University of New York Press, Albany

EU GPSR Authorised Representative:
Logos Europe, 9 rue Nicolas Poussin, 17000, La Rochelle, France
contact@logoseurope.eu

For information, contact State University of New York Press, Albany, NY
www.sunypress.edu

Library of Congress Cataloging-in-Publication Data

Name: Krell, David Farrell, author.
Title: This dagger, my heart : a novel / David Farrell Krell.
Description: Albany : State University of New York Press, [2025]. | Series:
    SUNY series in contemporary continental philosophy | Includes
    bibliographical references.
Identifiers: LCCN 2024060859 | ISBN 9798855803310 (hardcover : alk. paper) |
    ISBN 9798855803327 (ebook) | ISBN 9798855803334 (pbk. : alk. paper)
Subjects: LCSH: Günderode, Karoline von, 1780–1806—Fiction. | LCGFT:
    Biographical fiction. | Historical fiction. | Novels.
Classification: LCC PS3561.R423 T48 2025 | DDC 813/.54—dc23/eng/20250107
LC record available at https://lccn.loc.gov/2024060859

Detail of a photograph of the so-called "Heidelberg Miniature," now lost. It may be the cameo that Karoline von Günderrode sent to Friedrich Creuzer in Heidelberg seven months before her death. Although it has been assumed to be a portrait of her, the cameo (artist unknown) is in fact based closely on a stipple engraving by Francesco Bartolozzi (1728–1815) with the title "La Sainte Vierge."

For Barbara

Prologue

A lacerated heart stabs us like a knife that has been thrust
into our own heart. . . . When a cry of suffering
calls out to us, it stabs our soul.

—J. G. Herder, *Ideas Toward a Philosophy
of the History of Humankind*

How long does it take to tell the story of a life? It can be told in a few lines, taking just a few seconds, if the story recounts only the major turns of a life viewed from the outside. If the story recounts not only the major turns but also the minor twists, it will take longer. If the storyteller is gripped by all the twists and turns and even by the secret thoughts and half-revealed feelings that rise and subside in a life, recounting all of that would be the work of several lifetimes, even if the life in question were quite short. Neither I nor the reader has a lifetime or two to spare, so let me be brief, as she was.

Karoline von Günderrode—her family name is sometimes spelled with two *r*'s, sometimes with one—was born the eldest of six children to an aristocratic but impoverished family in Karlsruhe, Germany, in 1780. Her father, to whom she was close, died when she was six. Three of her sisters died of tuberculosis during their teenage years, and young Karoline nursed them up to the end. Before that, when Karoline was only seventeen, her mother had decided that she could not afford to keep all her children; she sent Karoline to an institution for unmarried aristocratic matrons, something like a convent, albeit less strict. Karoline hated it, and she traveled to stay with friends as often as she could. Much of her time she spent on study. Universities were not yet open to women, and so, with the help of mentors, she educated herself in the sciences, history, languages, and philosophy, especially the nature philosophy of F. W. J. Schelling. She also wrote poetry and pursued playwriting—indeed, when she was twenty-four years old, she published (under the nom de plume "Tian") two books of poems, plays, and sketches. A third book of poems and letters, *Melete*, was to be published in 1806, but after her death it was suppressed.

She fell in love at least twice, first with Carl von Savigny, a talented and handsome student of law, who had already befriended a number of important Romantic writers—among them, Clemens Brentano, Clemens' sister Bettine, and Achim von Arnim, whom Bettine later married. Bettine Brentano and Karoline became best friends. Much of what we know about Karoline comes from the memoir of her written decades later by Bettine Brentano von Arnim. Savigny, who had feelings for Karoline but was put off by her learning and her odd literature, chose to marry Bettine's older sister Gunda, a simpler sort of person. Karoline and Savigny remained friends, though he seems to have wished it could be more than that. She fell in love a second time with a professor of Greek literature and ancient Near Eastern and Indian mythologies, Friedrich Creuzer. Now, Creuzer and Savigny too were friends; Savigny even helped Creuzer financially during their student days. One wonders what Savigny felt about Karoline's love for Creuzer. One wonders too about the feelings others in the group had for Karoline—Achim von Arnim, who wrote about her in two of his exotic stories; Clemens Brentano, who was rather direct in expressing his admiration of her; and Clemens' sister Bettine, who seems to have loved Karoline passionately. As for Creuzer, he too certainly loved Karoline, although he was unwilling or unable to divorce his wife Sophie to remarry. Karoline and Sophie Creuzer struggled to remain on good terms with one another, as Sophie pondered whether to grant the divorce and her husband worried about the impact the love affair would have on his reputation and his Heidelberg professorship. Creuzer suffered a breakdown, and his friends worried he might die. As he began to convalesce, he broke off the relationship with Karoline by having yet another friend of his and Savigny's write a letter to a friend of Karoline's, a rather indirect method to terminate a relationship, but one that circumvented his having to confront Karoline directly. After intercepting that letter on the afternoon of July 26, 1806, Karoline walked to the edge of the Rhine River near the town of Winkel, where she was spending her holidays, and plunged a dagger through her heart.

She had owned the dagger for several years. She was twenty-six years old when she died.

•

They say—whoever they are and however they might know such a thing—that during the final seconds of conscious life, especially in cases of a suddenly impending demise, a person's entire life flashes by in memory. But I believe much more than that happens. In that instant of intense turbulence before the candle goes out, I imagine one witnesses dozens of lives flashing by, hears voices and sees visions from a distant time, receives more visitations from the remote past than one could have imagined one ever knew, all of it in something like a theatrical production with an enormous cast and all the personae declaiming at once. And not merely people you have known in your life, but also people you have only heard of or read about in books—the ancient Roman Lucretia turning her weapon on herself and so, they say, founding the Roman Republic; Julius Caesar and Brutus on their way to the senate near the end of that Republic; Shakespeare at the Globe or some other theater directing *Julius Caesar* or *Macbeth*; Socrates raising the cup of hemlock to his lips; Schelling wondering aloud whether God really must be a woman and why in all the world she created the universe instead of nothing at all—and even people you know nothing about, complete strangers from the spirit world who pepper you with poorly formulated questions that you struggle to answer but cannot, as in a troubled dream; and even, finally, the things of nature, rivers and trees, as well as things we say are lifeless, such as stones and household implements or articles of clothing and favorite books on the shelf—perhaps they too hurtle by us with extraordinary force and reveal something to us, so that our dying is as busy as our lives ever were and certainly much longer lasting, at least if time is not calculated in the usual ways. It is as though we were swept up in a powerful gyre, all things and we ourselves spinning madly as in a maelstrom that sucks us down to the seabed or a cyclone that catapults us into the upper air. I cannot prove any of this yet, but I mean to do so some day.

•

I have borrowed freely from Karoline's works and letters, as well as from the works and letters of her contemporaries, without citing sources. Nor have I shied from adding things I believe she or her contemporaries *might* have said. This is not a work of history but a collection of imagined points of view, not a biography but fragments of fiction, stained by all the sins of storytelling and marred by all the outrages of fiction. My only goal has been to be true to the outrage of her death.

The Cast of Characters
in the Order of Their Appearance

CLEMENS BRENTANO (1778–1842), poet and novelist, dependably desperate in his many loves, one of which is Karoline. Her feelings about him are mixed—ranging from admiration of his early poetry, through mild dislike of his person, to revulsion.

KAROLINE VON GÜNDERRODE (1780–1806), poet and philosopher.

BETTINE BRENTANO (1785–1859), a worshipful friend of Karoline's, later the wife of Achim von Arnim and the author of *Die Günderrode*, an epistolary memoir written more than thirty years after Karoline's death. Strangely, Bettine's memoir makes no mention of Karoline's death.

ACHIM VON ARNIM (1781–1831), co-author with Clemens Brentano of *Des Knaben Wunderhorn* ("The Youth's Magic Horn"), an influential collection of German folksongs; a poet and novelist, Arnim is a friend to Karoline. Her death affects him deeply. Two of his best known novellas, "Isabella of Egypt" and "Melück Maria Blainville" dwell on aspects of Karoline's person, character, and fate. "Melück" even takes its readers to that place on the Rhine where Karoline ended her life.

CARL VON SAVIGNY (1779–1861), eventually a renowned jurist in Berlin, is Karoline's first great love. He is at the center of a group of important Romantic writers, including the persons mentioned above. The circle often gathers at Savigny's bucolic summer estate, Trages, near the Main River, not far from Frankfurt and Hanau. One of Karoline's many visits to Trages, a particularly difficult visit for her, takes place in April 1804, when Savigny and Bettine's older sister Gunda marry.

SAPPHO (ca. 600 BCE), poetess of love on the isle of Lesbos. Karoline would have been bemused by the fact that some time after her death a critic proclaims her "the Sappho of German Romanticism."

FRIEDRICH CREUZER (1771–1858), an influential classical philologist at the University of Heidelberg, an expert in ancient languages, religions, and mythologies. Creuzer marries the widow of his former doctoral supervisor, a woman thirteen years his elder; he then falls hopelessly in love with Karoline, who is nine years younger than he, and she falls in love with him. Her pet name for him is Eusebio, derived from the Greek word for "piety." Creuzer shies from divorcing his wife Sophie, however, fearing the impact on his reputation and uncertain about whether to sacrifice the comforts of home life on the altar of Eros.

CARL DAUB (1765–1836), theologian, colleague and advisor to Creuzer. Daub, whose wife was a childhood friend of Karoline's, disapproves of Creuzer's passionate affair. Daub will write the letter that dissolves their relationship and ends Karoline's life.

YOUNG WERTHER, the central character of Goethe's novel *Die Leiden des jungen Werther* (1774, revised 1787). *The Sufferings of Young Werther* was one of Karoline's favorite books, a book she wanted to have with her at all times.

BRUNO, a code name (and one of the book titles) of the idealist philosopher Friedrich Wilhelm Joseph Schelling (1775–1854), Karoline's favorite thinker. She fills a notebook with detailed observations on Schelling's philosophy of nature.

BONAVENTURA, pseudonym of August Klingemann (1777–1831), the presumed author of *Nightwatches*, published in 1804–5, a darkly satirical response to German Idealism and Romanticism. He serves as a kind of foil to "Bruno." Whether Karoline actually read Klingemann's (or "Bonaventura's") book is unknown, but she surely entertains a number of its darkest suspicions.

JOHANN WOLFGANG VON GOETHE (1749–1832) never meets Karoline, but he reads with interest her first book of poems and plays. Bettine

Brentano later tells Goethe about this beloved friend of her youth, one of whose favorite fictions, to repeat, was Goethe's *The Sufferings of Young Werther*.

THE CONFESSOR. An early Church Father reminiscent of Augustine of Hippo, the Confessor responds to the legend of the venerated Roman heroine Lucretia. Lucretia, who lived in old Rome during the reign of kings, that is, before the birth of the Republic, was raped by Tarquin, a prince of Rome. Lucretia then stabbed herself through the heart. Her rape and her death are said to have so enraged the citizens of Rome that they banished the Tarquin family and instituted the Roman republic. The Confessor, however, has doubts about Lucretia.

HERACLITUS OF EPHESUS (ca. 550–480 BCE), called the Obscure, is a favorite philosopher of Karoline's. He is notorious for his love of paradox—the way up is the way down, he was wont to say—and for his devotion to the "Logos" and to "ever-living fire."

EMPEDOCLES OF ACRAGAS (ca. 500–430 BCE), the thinker of Love and Strife in the vortex of the world, is another favorite of Karoline's. A relatively large number of lines from Empedocles' philosophical poems survives. Yet another poet cherished by Karoline, Friedrich Hölderlin (1770–1843), wrote three versions of a tragedy titled *The Death of Empedocles*.

THE SURGEON. It is reported that Karoline receives instructions from a surgeon on how to stab oneself successfully through the heart, which is protected by the sternum, the ribs, and a considerable amount of muscle tissue, so that it is not so easy of access.

ZARDUSCHT, an ancient Persian prophet who lived as early as the ninth or as late as the seventh century of the ancient era. Creuzer introduces Karoline to the prophet as the teacher of good and evil. Yet Karoline finds other aspects of the lore surrounding Zarduscht (known also as Zoroaster or Zarathustra) more intriguing, for he is said to have been "born posthumously."

SOPHIE CREUZER (1758–1831), wife of Friedrich Creuzer, referred to as the Benefactress by her husband and Karoline alike. Sophie at first agrees to a divorce, feeling the force of her husband's passion for Karoline, but then changes her mind.

THE NIGHTWATCH, called in the early morning hours of July 27, 1806, to the scene of Karoline's suicide, which had occurred some twelve hours earlier, entertains severe doubts about her death. He is keen to preserve the evidence.

FATHER ISINGER. Johann Michael Isinger (1758–1809), a Catholic priest and pastor of St. Walburga's church in Winkel-on-Rhine, buries Karoline's remains in the churchyard and carries out her last wishes, of which he has somehow been apprised. Isinger's superiors are scandalized: Karoline was not a Catholic, and she had killed herself—two irremediable grounds for denying her burial at St. Walburga's. Yet that is where she is buried and that is where Isinger allows a memorial plaque to be erected to her. It is as though he had known her.

MELETE (ἡ μελέτη) means, in ancient Greek, "care taken" or "attention paid" to a thing, especially in the sense of "study" and "the pursuit of knowledge." Karoline, under the influence of Creuzer, chooses this word as the title of her last book of poems and letters. Creuzer, fearing that he will be recognized as the lover Eusebio in the book, manages to suppress it. Only one copy of the book's page proofs survives, copied out by a jurist friend of the Brentanos and Savigny.

Finally, it is commonly believed that material things do not speak, but the problem evidently lies with the limited range of human hearing. Some things are actually quite articulate. In the present case, Trages, the Savigny summer estate, the Rhine River, flocks of songbirds, a pair of white slippers, a novel, and a dagger share their thoughts with us.

I

Clemens Brentano

I was quite taken with her when I first met her. And I never got over that first surge of interest—not exactly a passion, yet something close to that, something like a head-spinning circle dance, at least in my imagination, where all the passions join hands. I met her in Marburg on a day in mid-May 1802. That evening I wrote her a little note. There is a touch of springtime folly in it.

—Good night, you sweet angel! Ah, are you the one, or are you not? If you are, then open all the arteries of your white body so that hot foaming blood may jet from a thousand delightful fountains, that's the way I want to see you, and I will drink from those myriad sources, imbibing your blood to the point of intoxication so that I can lament your death in a frenzy of shouts, weeping back into you all your blood and my own admixed with tears until your heart begins to beat again and you commence to trust me since my blood comes alive in your very pulse.—Oh, if you knew me you would lose the courage to love me, because you cannot grasp who I am, since you don't know me.—I know an infinite number of things, such that my heart explodes when I try to say them, but speaking is a slow martyrdom to the death, and were you to lie with me but one night you would cause my love to rise to a slow boil on your warm breasts and you would know everything that I know and you would no longer need to be terrified of all the things I dare to say simply because I want to say them. You truly dear child, youth is tender, and one cannot converse with it. Youth should take lessons from life. Oh, you dear young thing, may I not teach you? It's true, is it not, that you don't love me? Yes, that's what people generally do, and you should do the same, for you doubtless also believe that what people know is evil and what is kept secret is good. Your head may well spin because of these words of mine, for you are fond of all sorts of things you shouldn't be, oh, all you poor dear two-legged angels in hell, and you, dear Günderrode, in a convent for girls, how much I love you all, all you devils and angels, my heart is no poor soul. I am writing all this in a sweetly spinning rapture, the moonlit night and the spring have not been shy about ravishing me with the sweet labors of love and, lest my consciousness of such voluptuosity lose itself, they have caused the sighs of love to break in echoes on my breast. And as the sighs embraced one another they transformed themselves into a golden, bittersweet, voluptuous snake that wrapped me round in the vital pulsating crushing upward-tending coils of its body, such that I was perched on a mountaintop peering down into the outspread valley below that imposed itself on my heart like a little mound of its own, and I tore off my clothes so that the embrace would be more chaste, when, as sudden and electric as lightning, the golden snake bit into my heart and twisted itself about my entire body, writhing in pleasure, poisoning me with divine love, and another life entered mine, flowing through my arteries and my marrow whose resistance surrendered everything, and the viper slithered into the wound it had opened and now it coils joyously and lovingly about my heart, and what I possess is much too much; thus I bite into my own arteries, wanting to give this much-too-much back to you, but this is what *you* should have done, it was for *you* to suck. Do not open your arteries, then, tender Günderrode, I will bite them open for you. Oh, I would be an Arabian steed, why not, if I had you here. And here beside me you would see such splendid nuptials celebrated. The moonlit night and spring would be their echo, the echo I was for them—. (If you do not understand me, write me and tell me so, that I may cease writing altogether.)

Write me somewhat rational letters, my dear angel, and if you can love me, do it, not a droplet of such sweet wine should go to waste. I drink your health with every glimpse of spring and my every thought of you is the good health that I toast to the spring. If you are lovable then of course I must love you, that is the very essence of love, the essence of my essence, as of your essence. Fare ye well, and have the courage to weep for this alone, that you are with me not in the flesh but only in my thoughts, although the two are one, and only in holy communion are we with God, for every Word must become flesh, including the Word of love.

Clemens Brentano

What sort of effect does this letter have on you, ma petite Günderrode? I fear you will pretend to be much smarter or much dumber than you really are, don't be a child, my child, and learn how to live, which is to say, concern yourself with God alone.

Karoline

I was twenty-two when I received this missive from Clemens. I was still hopelessly in love with Savigny, not Clemens, and more in love with Clemens' sister Bettine than with her brother the amorous vampire. Sucking the blood of virgins, he himself seems to have suffered snakebite while agallop on Arabian steeds, spying down on the moonlit mounds and valleys below, hearing the Word of God and all the echoes of spring and suck—what was a girl to make of this whirligig from a man she scarcely knew? I answered the letter, of course. Civility demanded it.

—Dear Sir! After perusing your letter I had a very strange reaction; yet it was more a matter of thought than emotion. For it seemed to me, and seems to me still, that this letter of yours was not written for me. Thus I deprive myself of it. Yet it is no disingenuous artifice that I react this way; it occurred to me quite naturally. Indeed, I understand the moment in which you wrote to me. Yet I have not made any progress beyond understanding at least some little bit of these moments of your own. I know nothing about their context and their basic tonality. It seems to me that you have several souls in you. Whenever one of those souls begins to please me it up and vanishes, and along comes another one to take its place. I do not recognize the new one. I gape at it in astonishment. However, I do not want to contemplate all your souls, since I trust only one of them, and that one is a frightened little boy who has been cast out into the street. The poor child is now more perplexed than ever, for it cannot find its way back home.

As for the rest, I cannot really write you about myself. I perused your earlier letter to Bettine on the theme of truth, and it brought me much joy; its insights into things that had been obscure and undecidable for me made me richer.

Bettine will enclose this letter of mine with one from her. I have not seen her for such a long time nor has she written me as she promised she would.

As for me, I am more diligent. I am sketching again. In short, I am following all your reasonable counsels.

Your Karoline.

Bettine

Günderrode! I look back now across decades and I see her. I can almost smell her—the scent of spring flowers. She was so gentle, so mellow in all her traits, so like a little girl, a lithe little blonde girl roaming over high mountain meadows. As it was, her hair was dark brown, almost black, but her eyes were bright blue, and they had the longest curled lashes. When you looked into those eyes you knew you would never find your way out again. You were lost. Or found. I am still lost after all these years, and after all these years she finds me constant.

When she laughed it was not some raucous yawp, as with me, but more like the cooing of a turtledove expressing pleasure and evident good cheer. She did not flounce about, as other people do, so much as glide or drift—if you can understand what I mean by that. Her dress, no matter how austere because of the prison house of old ladies where she lived, was a coverlet that wrapped her body round in flattering folds. That's because her movements were so graceful. She was tall. I looked up to her. We all looked up to her. Her figure was too flowing, too graceful to be captured by the word *slender*. She was shy. That is to say, she was friendly but much too reticent to make her presence felt in society.

She was declared an old maid at age seventeen. Her mother could not afford to keep her at home, or so she said, sending her off to a Matrons' Residence in Frankfurt. It might as well have been a convent. The ladies were forbidden to attend the theater—and Karoline a playwright!—they weren't allowed to dance—and Karoline a dancer! She showed me the regulations, I nearly fainted.

> The women should refrain from all godless, luxuriant, and vulgar conversation. They must pay close attention that the entire house and their particular quarters are kept clean and tidy. Furthermore, it is forbidden to entertain guests apart from the closest family members, and only in cases of emergency may male visitors be received. Rather, the residents should engage in prayer and extensive Bible study, devoting the remaining time to household

chores and domestic pursuits. In short, they must see to it that they lead a life of exemplary seclusion.

This seemed to me a recipe for insanity—and Karoline agreed with me. She was happy to be alone, to read and study, but she was anything but an anchorite.

We would dress up when I visited her. She loved the new fashion, the styles of the Revolution. Actually, the new fashion was antique Greek, *à la camise*, dispensing with the *bustier* and the crinoline behind, nothing but a long, fine muslin dress cut square above the bust. We would dance! She insisted on being the man, and so I called her Günter! But especially in that muslin dress, she made an absurd man. She pirouetted like a goddess. That is what she looked like, and that is what she was to me. A goddess!

She had rooms on the ground floor of the Residence, opening onto the garden, and that is where we loved to be. Otherwise, the old ladies would have driven us both batty. We played most of our games in that garden. Only the bleakest winter days drove us inside, where we hovered around the stove. She was twenty-four when we grew close. I was only nineteen, but an entire lifetime sillier. I used to clamber up the tree in the garden just to scare her.

—Come down! You'll fall! Please, please come down! she would cry.

Such a beautiful woman! I liked it best when our games were done and I could lay my head in her lap and she would read to me. Hölderlin's *Hyperion*, Novalis's *Ofterdingen*, Schlegel's *Lucinde*. Or she would teach me about Plato and Heraclitus and Empedocles, scolding me because I was too lazy to read, especially the soporific modern philosophers, who really did put me to sleep. Still, those were the happiest moments of my life, her reading to me. And if I were to raise my head and kiss the breast that was barely hiding beneath the muslin, she would gently chide me—*don't be so silly!*—and I would settle back into her lap. But I was always silly, I never stopped being silly, she made me silly with love, and I ceased being silly only when she died.

Karoline

Clemens became and remained my naughty boy. He taught me an important lesson, which was that the higher the value of a banknote the easier it is to counterfeit. Not that he was guilty of premeditated counterfeiting. He had no more awareness of what he was doing than I did. Because love is the supreme value, it lends itself most readily to deception. He taught me that lesson, and I should be grateful to him. But I was a miserable pupil, and I immediately forgot the lesson.

I told Clemens I could say nothing about myself, but that was because my description of him—the frightened child cast into the street and unable to find his way back home—said everything essential about myself. Boy or girl makes no difference, at least in this respect. We are all children terrified by the unfeeling world that affronts us. We crouch at the edge of our beds and wish we could sink back under the covers and not have to face it. I do have to admit that some children are more obnoxious than others, but by and large we are all terrified and piteous creatures.

I was six when they carried my father's coffin out of the house in Hanau. I was left with my four younger sisters, a baby brother, and a feckless mother. Now three of those sisters are dead—Louise, Amalie, and my darling Charlotte—and the sister who meant the least to me married and moved away. That leaves young Hector and an incompetent mother who is enamored of the theater and who flirts with the tutor of the children she never really loved and who is dipping into my paternal inheritance. She showed me the door when I was seventeen, sent me to a house for rich old maids in Frankfurt, as much a nunnery as anything else. Here I bide my time, dressed from top to toe in somber gray and black, a deplorable habit, grateful only for my ground floor apartment and the garden. Were it not for the garden I would already have gone to join my sisters and my father.

Strange that father's name was Hector, a bit silly, really. He gave that name to my sole brother as well. The hero of Troy? My father's only heroism shone forth in his library—but then he opened that library to me. He sat me on his knee and read to me from Homer's *Iliad* and *Odyssey* or Plutarch's *Lives*, explaining to me all the things I could not understand.

He taught me how to read and write and what to write about. Life stories. Biographies. Histories of a life and a death.

I never really left that library, but I did expand my reading a bit. Philosophers like Herder and Schelling, Schelling above all others, since no one is like him—his devotion to nature is total. Poets like Novalis, who died at twenty-eight, and dear Hölderlin, who still lives on, if you can call that a life. He used to be my secret neighbor. I spied on him and his Diotima.

What do I read? Everything that stirs the heart's blood, replenishing it and filling it with extraordinary adventures, everything that urges the reader to the forefront of perfection. And so, I have found my joy in reading the lives and thoughts of others, dreaming of the possibility of creating such a life for myself. Yet it has always seemed to me that one can never create a complete human being; one invents only a single side, an aspect, a facet, so that the complexity of human existence is never aptly portrayed. Really to see and to understand this limitation is what has made me so interested in history. Mohammed crouching on the edge of his pallet, not knowing whether he will sink back in torpor or go forth. Ossian trembling before plucking his lyre and singing the Celtic heroes.

And then we others, we contemporaries. Clemens. Bettine. Achim. Savigny. Creuzer. Karoline. All the frightened children, all the castaways who cannot find their way back home.

The Dagger

Double-edged, yes, and much more modest in length than a sword or rapier. Yet neither my edges nor my length is the point. The point is my point. No man's flesh can withstand it. My *punctum* is puncture. Yet I am, after a long life of service, about to be abused.

I am keeping my temper about it. I was tempered in the hottest fires of the forge and in the coldest waters of the streams high in the mountains west of Damascus. I was made in fresh memory of the heroic days when I would have pierced the heart of a Christian dog or a Frankish or Saxon swine, warriors of the devil—what in the world does this slip of a girl think she is doing with me? It was degrading enough to be a slave of merchants for centuries, sold at fairs from east to west like chattel, treated like a trinket and a tool for opening lilac-scented envelopes. But this? To bend to the will of a woman?

I bend to no one. I was not made for this. Yes, I have a handle, silver studded and masterfully worked, of the hardest wood petrified by the blood of many a Crusader, as I like to imagine. But behold the hand that holds me now.

Alabaster. A minute hand, its fingers stems of daffodils. Tremulous. I do not know if I can keep my temper. But God is with me. God is in me, and God is of me. God is heavy metal, you see. No amount of oxygen will corrode or even stain me. Oxygen is of the devil. This woman and all her kind, males as well as females, breathe oxygen until it eats holes in the spongy tissue of their lungs and the fibers wither away and they are altogether consumed. I have no lungs. I puncture lungs. I am breathtaking. I am sudden. I am double-edged but irreversible.

Oxygen does not faze me, nor water. I could lie buried at the bottom of a river or lie in the wet grass on a riverbank and emerge eons later after the grass and the river alike have dried to annihilation and my sheen still would shine. My handle might be the worse for wear, water too is of the devil, at least by half, and even the most hardened woody fibers eventually succumb to moist corruption. For wood was once alive and of the devil's part.

I am clairvoyant, as most things are. I can see it now, as plain as day. I can feel it. The horrid moisture of the grass, the nearby river, and that trembling alabaster palm. The vision offends me. But I pull myself together. I reflect on the past glories of my kind and I preserve my temper. I steel myself.

What does this poor fool think she is doing? The two of us should spurn intimacy. We were not made for each other.

Karoline

This is my body. I could scarcely hear or read those words, much less repeat them. Only a god dare say them—that was the proof. For me, at least when I was in a crowd, it was always a matter of stepping back two or three paces out of my body. I had been told I was beautiful, my father founded that myth, as every father does for every daughter. Lisette and my other friends confirmed it, however, and Bettine insisted on it, even if I never believed them. There were some uncanny moments, I confess, when I seemed to see it and even acknowledge it as undeniable. When I was eighteen, I drew two sketches for my little story about the nymph Calypso. I recently examined some details of the first sketch, which shows Calypso hunting with her companion Tillina.

I had given the nymph my long legs. I pinned her chiton high so that everyone could see the slender thighs and calves, the delicate feet. I also opened her garment at the top, as though she were an Amazon. I gave her my high breast and my finely focused nipple—as though these were universal traits—without being aware that they were my own. It turned out that I was the nymph, even though I felt more like her timid companion, whose gaze is forever downcast, her whole manner subservient. Even Tillina is beautiful, as she gazes longingly at Calypso's legs, believing that she herself is nothing. Tillina is a near rhyme of Bettine, and I suppose the two of us would have wrangled about who was the goddess and who the acolyte, who the nymph and who the wallflower, each of us proclaiming the divinity of the other.

—*This is* your *body*, we would have insisted.

I suppose that when my sisters became ill and slowly deteriorated before my eyes I stepped even farther out of my own body, the tortured companion of my soul. An unrelieved pressure in my chest, trouble swallowing, headaches, eyes weakening day by day: this could not end well. I could not bear to think of my lungs or stomach or spleen or any other organ. I preferred to be a ragdoll stuffed with horsehair or cotton, not a living dying organism. Even when I melted in the company of some young man or woman, when I learned that my organs were flammable, malleable, molten, I could not accept the flesh. That began to change—at least in my mind—when I read Schelling's nature books, which said that the flesh itself was magnetized and electrified by a materializing deity. Otherwise, the talk of Creation made no sense. If God had made all out of nothing, then everything would consist of nothing, and nothing would have been made. If She made it all out of what was available to Her, which was Herself, since in the beginning She was utterly alone, then Creation is the living All, and her heart and all her organs are molten and electric.

My feelings about the body, my body, every body, have not changed all that much since I first read him, but I continue to read. I try to learn. I try to make my way to the forefront of perfection. Some day, even in a crowd, I may not need to step out of myself and hide behind the curtain.

This is my body, yes, but this is my *blood*? Those words I have never read or heard spoken without feeling faint. The mere mention of blood, to say nothing of the sight of it—no, no, I am one of those skittish women you hear about. You would think that dealing with the lunar phases, as every woman must, would have accustomed me to it, but no, not even that helps.

Not long ago the visiting physician informed me that my arteries were overfull and portended the onset of nerve fever—I, like virtually all the other women in the Residence, would have to undergo a bloodletting. He would open a vein in us all. I flew into a panic. I wrote to Bettine that my anxiety about it was making me sick, that when I thought of it spilling out of me I felt nauseous, paralyzed, about to swoon. She wrote me back immediately—*Don't you do it! Don't you let him do it!* She warned me that I might die, or that I might do endless harm to my soul if I allowed it, that bloodletting would deprive my posterity—a bizarre notion to me—of every chance at full-blooded heroism.

I was already in a speeding post-coach when the sanguinary surgeon arrived at the Residence, and I stayed away for a week, just to be certain. It was a wonderful week, not very heroic, but I was happy to have escaped with my life.

Achim von Arnim

As I was disembarking, I saw them standing arm in arm on the wharf. Clemens had told me his sister and her best friend would be at the river dock to meet me. They introduced themselves proudly as soul sisters, but there was absolutely no family likeness between them. The one was all effervescence, the other very still waters; the one a Lambrusco, the other a Romagna red; the one an acrobat, the other a ballerina; the one an open book, the other a locked diary, a sealed codicil, an encryption. My preference? I was always a serious person.

The three of us took a long hike through the glorious countryside. Late in the afternoon a rainstorm surprised us. Coup de foudre! We were drenched, the younger one a drowned puppy, the older one, the taller one, a statue in some Greek collection, cleansed but otherwise unaltered. We found rooms at a nearby inn and we dried out; we were able to borrow some clean but ill-fitting clothing. One of the two was a Sancho Panza, the other an Ottilie or Ophelia. That evening we talked and laughed ourselves to sheer exhaustion; we made up stories and played charades till long after dark.

Then the god Hypnos, the brother of Death, called to us. Through the paper-thin wall I could hear them in the next room arguing about which of the two I would choose. I chose neither of them—at least not until one of the two withdrew from the competition. It was not merely that time had to pass before I finally could and did choose; it was that eternity had to intervene before I could act.

I was not sure whether I would ever be able to write about her. Eventually I had to wonder whether I would ever be able to write about anyone else. The prophetess, the sorceress, the captor and keeper of hearts. Such as mine.

Karoline

The garden at the Residence abutted another much larger and more splendid garden, that of the Gontard estate, White Hart. I often went there to spy through the hedges. The two of them would go strolling through the garden, sometimes with the children, sometimes alone. I thought at first he was her husband, they were so at ease together, but one of the ladies at the Residence told me that her husband stayed at the bank all day long. I concluded that it must be the children's tutor she was walking with, and when I learned the tutor's name I could not believe my good luck. I went more and more often to the hedge. I crouched and I observed.

Madame Gontard was as beautiful as I wish I could have been, let *regal* be my word. She was clearly a queen or a priestess. She was his Diotima, after all! Her hair was dark, like my own, but thicker and all curls, luxuriant locks ruffled by the wind. But the truth is that he was more beautiful than she. I ate him with my eyes. Hölderlin! My elderberry!

I had seen an issue of *Thalia* in my friend Lisette's library. I borrowed it and devoured his "Fragment of Hyperion" before I knew anything about him. He calls Diotima *Melite* there. I would do a variation on that later in my life. And then the two volumes of the completed *Hyperion* appeared, and I got hold of them both and read one after the other. Indeed, I read them through twice, both forward and back and up and down. They formed the core of all my thinking and feeling. *Every deed and every thought of humankind over the millennia—what are they when measured against a single instant of love? But love is also nature at its most successful, the most divinely beautiful thing in nature!* In the moment of Hyperion's loneliest loneliness She appears to him—*and in the midst of sighing Chaos she appeared to me: Urania*—wondrous, holy, a priestess of love from Zeus's oracle at Dodona, woven out of light and sweet fragrance and Plato. She is keen intelligence, yet she is tender of heart. She is fragile, yet she has the strength to love without reserve. She dies at the outset of the novel, already in the first volume; in fact, she is always already gone, and Hyperion is in mourning from the outset to the end. *Do you hear me? Do you hear me? Diotima's grave! My heart grew still, and my love was interred with the dead woman I loved.* I could have been that for him! I mean for Hölderlin himself. Only a boxwood hedge separated my life from his. The heady fragrance of that hedge and the priestess with her children. I breathed it all in.

Years later Bettine wrote to say she had hatched a plan for us to visit him. Sinclair had told her that Hölderlin was ill—and that he was living in Homburg vor der Höhe, just north of Frankfurt. We would visit him, Bettine and I, and we would cure him of whatever ailed him! Bettine's eldest brother and guardian, Franz, forbade her to go, of course, said she had the Saint Vitus dance. That wasn't far off the mark.

—What?! You want to visit a madman? Do you want to go crazy too? You are a lightning rod for lunacy!

Bettine was ready to risk it if I would accompany her. We would pretend that we were going to visit her sick grandmother in Hanau. Her grandmother would cooperate with the plan, and we would slip off to Homburg. People in Frankfurt were saying terrible things about Hölderlin—that he had gone mad with guilt over his affair with Madame Gontard, an affair that had robbed her of her life and him of his sanity. But Bettine had an apt response, as she always did.

—Why say these terrible things about him just because he loved a woman so he could write *Hyperion*?

Whether or not out of guilt, Hölderlin was clearly unwell. Princess Auguste had given him a Hammerklavier as thanks for his having dedicated to her his Sophocles translations, but he severed a number of its strings, not all of them but some of them, so that several keys went click-clack instead of striking their assigned tone. It was driving the neighbors to distraction. Click-clack, click-clack. They wanted him committed. That crippled instrument was an emblem of his soul, said Bettine, and we would repair them both. We would mend the strings.

She was always plotting adventures, dear Bettine, but none of them more adventurous than that one. And I would have given anything to see him, if I thought we could help him. But it was not only Franz who gave me pause. Bettine herself had been unwell all that spring. I had nursed her back to health—yet another sister in mortal danger! I could not bear the thought of her dying, and she was still a bundle of Saint Vitus nerves. I talked it over with all our friends and with Sinclair as well. For her to see the poet in his reported state would certainly not help her. Sinclair was certain the visit would help the poet, but I was unsure of that as well. I remembered what Hölderlin had imagined Diotima saying to her lover: *Dear—dear Hyperion! You are surely a difficult person to help. . . . You didn't want a human being, believe me, you wanted a world.*

17

I still can smell that peppery boxwood hedge at White Hart. I still feel the longing I felt there. But I have found another garden, another Hyperion, and we will make our own children. But, oh, the god in us is forever lonely, forever poverty stricken, forever craving and languishing. *We are nothing. What we seek is everything. It must be outed, the deeply held secret that will grant me life or death!*

The Rhine

Evening falls, the hour of briefest blue, but I can find my way northward even in the dark. At least that is what I have always believed. Yet the west has distracted me and lured me off course for quite a while now, as it did back in the beginning, during the eon of my youth. I wanted to meet the rising sun, to flow from the Alps all the way to Asia, with the setting sun at my heels. But there were impediments. I tried to move mountains, but the mountains moved me. And so I found myself committed for a time to the Occident. I went west. I struggled against that destiny, tried to turn about, but I succeeded only halfway at Basel and wound up heading toward the Hyperborean north. Until hard rock forced me westward once again.

These are pleasant villages nonetheless, the hills on either side of me garlanded with grapes. The villagers are busy in the vineyards, busy in the towns, busy on the road, busy on my rippled surface, but unaware of my undertow. Each summer the boys of the towns offer me one of their own in unwitting sacrifice. Eddies and long-legged flies on the surface, irresistible surge below. My true currents are darkly deep, their rush uncanny. You cannot step twice into what I am. You cannot step even once into what I am. Here today, gone today.

And so my advice to you is that you sing your Lorelei-Lied and do your best with what is yours for the time being. As for me, life is all Heraclitean flow.

Sometimes I am sluggish, I admit it. I dally and delay, I shilly-shally and I eddy. I hug the shore as though someone were waiting for me there. A rendezvous. When I pass the ragged elderberry bushes beneath the willow grove the songbirds mock me.

—What's this, O Father Rhine? You doze and dream in a daze, rapt to yourself alone, wrapped up in yourself? You drift along this silted shore, giving way to every fallen branch and rock? Heed your origin! You are the son of Okeanos, you are a scion of Titans!

Their remonstrance stings my breast, and yet these are words of love, well-meaning, full of solicitude. They remind me of the ancient father of all rivers and of all my brothers and sisters around the globe. A surge deep below my surface gets me going, I remember my power and my sovereignty.

Mocking the rocks and the wrack at every turn, I hurry on, I break my chains, no more fetters, no more manacles! Enraged, I toss them behind me. I make waves. They slap the shore, startle the elderberry bush birds. My voice, the voice of a son of gods, echoes in the mountains. The forests perk up and hearken, the gorge ahead of me hears the herald's cry, and the bosom of the earth shudders again in ecstasy.

Here I come! As in spring, when fragrant greenery greets the dawn, I am unstoppable life. I flow toward the immortals. Sorry, can't stay, cannot bide, neither here nor there, I won't stop till, like a child running to its father, I am finally snatched up in his arms!

Karoline

Sometimes in my walks along the river's edge I stop near an elderberry patch beneath the overarching willows. I sit amid shoots of dark ivy as the willows weep and the chickadees chatter. They flutter, disturbed at their feasting or lovemaking, but soon they settle down, having recognized a sister. I'm at the gateway of a beech and willow forest here, some of the willows tiptoeing all the way down to the water's edge. Some refuse to stop and they get their feet wet. The birds in the bushes twitter. I can almost make out what they are saying.

—Golden midday! Oh, if only we could fly this noon all the way to the river's Alpine source! The water comes tripping down two rocky stairways there, down from the fortress of mountains built by gods, the celestial ones!

I hear the birds and I want to fly with them. That is who I want to be! No matter how pusillanimous I have been all my life and still am, no matter how deluded I may be, I want to fly!

—The ancient peoples tell us their hoary secrets, chirp the birds. The ancient ones tell us of something like a fate or a destiny that comes tripping down the twin stairways.

The birds and I think of Scandinavia and Ireland and Scotland, the land of my Ossian, Old Hibernia; or we dream of the shores of the Peloponnesus, everywhere where rivers run. This one, our Rhine, starts amid the silvery peaks above forests of pine and fir. The rocky faces peer down beyond the pines into the coldest abysses below. Listen! You can hear the wailing of the unborn river. He rages against his own parents, mother Earth and father Thunder. That is to say, you could hear his rage if, alone among mortals, who generally shun the dark and dank dungeon, you ventured there. The demigod churns in his chains and he rages. He wants out!

Such was the voice of the noblest of streams, the freeborn Rhine. He hoped for a destiny different from that of his brothers, the Tessin and the Rhone, and he left them behind, impatient for Asia. That is where his kinglike soul wanted to go. But when you wish for something that counters your destiny, that wish is simply a misunderstanding. And the sons of gods are as blind as everyone else, perhaps the least insightful of us all. Human beings at least know where to build their houses and where their animals will find rich pasturage; what we don't know, as the river too does not know it, is where the inexperienced soul must travel. Riddles pop up on all sides. Even the poets and singers cannot unravel their sense.

—For as you began, that's the way you'll stay, sing the birds. You, with all your rage against progenitors and siblings alike, bull-headed and blind, O Rhine, misunderstanding everything. We are shaped by calamity, at least to some degree, and we are formed too by the way we are brought up. Yet what is most decisive is our birth and the beam of light that happens to shine on the newborn. *Fortuna primigenia*. Could there be anyone—preserving his freedom his whole life long, fulfilling his heart's desires, born from such heights—anyone else like you, O Rhine, born so propitiously and from such a high and holy womb?

That is why my poems merely mew and murmur, whereas when the river talks it's like a shout. He is not like other infants, he won't be swaddled, won't be weepy, and if the willows along the shoreline crowd him close and the banks twist and turn and try to fence him in, he'll tear right through them! Like Herakles, he'll laugh and rip apart the constrictors, sweeping them away in his current! And if something greater does not rise to tame him, he'll furrow the earth, affright the forests, and cajole the mountains! He is like lightning! That is who I want to be. No matter how I began. No matter how anemic that beam of light on my birth may have been. No matter how deluded I may be. I flex my arm and I write!

The White Slippers

Conformity is almost a bad word these days. Everyone says one should do one's best to avoid it. Yet our entire life is one of conformity—of conforming to the foot. We were made on a straight last, you see, so that the right-left orientation has no relevance for us. Kant would have been terribly confused to confront us: his entire system depended on knowing through unthinking sensuous apprehension right from left. He would have been dumbfounded to see us in our initial state. He would have preferred to go barefoot.

Karoline was not confused for a single moment. She was careful to decide from the very first day which one of us would go where, and we conformed to her wish from that day forward. To be intimate with those hyacinthine feet has been such a privilege! Such a sweet bouquet! An associate of hers says that Karoline does not walk about like other people but hovers and glides from place to place like a phantom—an absurd conceit, to be sure, but she is possessed of a certain *legerdepied*, as it were, yes, she is a dancer. When we contemplate what others of our kind have to put up with, the vulgarity and the ferment, we are humbled and gratified. Life is good!

We have no heel to speak of, but that is due to the excellence of our Revolutionary times. A generation ago, fine ladies were all in heels, to show that their birth had elevated them over the rabble. They tortured their feet with bunions and cramped and crossed toes horribly bent to the outer side, all but crippling themselves to put on aristocratic airs. Many of those fine ladies were recently beheaded. Women nowadays have determined to keep their heads, and so they have beheeled themselves, so to speak. *Égalité et sororité!*

Our uppers consist entirely of snow white linen spun from the finest flax cultivated by canny Hibernian Celts. Amber waves of flax from our ancestral fields are harvested in late summer, skillfully retted and broken to bast, the short, sturdy fibers selected for our body—which must carry the entire weight of the chosen person—and then spun, given a hot bath, reeled wet onto bobbins, and dried. After that drying we prefer to *stay* dry. We would not say that we suffer from hydrophobia, but we are hypersensitive to moisture. We possess a dry soul, the dream of the old philosophers. Our outsole is of beaten Irish straw, and once it gets wet, days will have to pass

23

until we can be worn again without danger of catarrh or even pneumonia. We avoid rainfall. We have an aversion to puddles.

We are summer slippers, then, sisters to the Zephyr breeze and friends to the mild airs that encourage the shedding of unwieldy winter footwear. Behold! She bends over us now. She wears a stunning ankle-length red dress that buttons down the front, the ruffle of her white chemise barely visible at the Florentine neckline, not so very plunging, both dress and chemise made of the longer, softer linen fibers. We are altogether a glory of linen! Her slender fingers gather the twined linen laces that meander and meet and cross from eyelet to eyelet on either side. She pulls the laces taut at the eyestays so that our uppers close securely over the wagging tongue that extends from vamp to throat, and our soft counter firmly embraces her shapely heels. We sport no Achilles tab, but we do not need it, we are not marching off to Troy! We are out for a stroll. Perhaps some friends will join us!

The hour is a bit late, later than usual, but it is high summer and the morning dew has long since evaporated, so that we will stay dry. Life is good!

Karoline

Bettine writes me about Sinclair's visit with Hölderlin in Homburg. The poet is still caught up in his Sophocles translations even now that they have been published. If Sophocles wanders amid unthinkable things—Oedipus murdering his father and bedding his mother, Antigone fusing brother with father and hoping to bed them both in the underworld—Hölderlin appears to be adrift in that same realm of shades. Sinclair paints a wretched portrait of him declaiming in hymns and sibylline oracles, confusing the date and even his name, then suddenly losing the thread, lapsing into silence. Of course, Sinclair is no poet, and Bettine is a chickadee trying to imitate a soaring eagle. She pecks at the seeds the poet has scattered across the tragic weft of time, but she has no idea about the high fruit whence they have fallen. She did force me to go back to Hölderlin's own notes on Oedipus and Antigone, which showed me that I too am less eagle than songbird.

The eagle is language itself, and we featherless bipeds are slaves to it—so much is true. Bettine hopes that *rhythm* will make the song comprehensible to us and liberate us from our servitude, but I am not sure whether she or I understand what he means by rhythm or tragic transport or caesura, to say nothing of the counterrhythmic interruption—O ye good gods in heaven and on earth! enlighten me! The only thing that seems certain is that tragedy is about death-in-life, the suffering organs of a body wrestling with god, and that when the characters in Sophocles' tragedies speak, their words are murderous. When we moderns speak, our words are merely mortifying.

Hölderlin. My elderberry. My Hyperion. He is now a secretly laboring soul. It is a great good fortune—for him and for us—that we did not visit him in his labyrinth. Our chatter would only have distracted him from the divine distraction to which he has been driven. What can help him? *It is a great help to the secretly laboring soul that at the summit of consciousness the soul evades consciousness, and before the soul can actually grasp the god who is present, it goes to encounter that god with bold words, even blasphemy, and in this way it preserves the holy and the living possibility of spirit.*

Neither Bettine nor I have bold enough words. She is too fidgety, I too timid. She is right to say that Hölderlin is holy to me because of that boldness. His heroism of love is more divine than all the pious prattle that

25

surrounds us. But this deity that we go to meet, if only with words of sacrilege in our teeth, who or what is it? If I am not mistaken, and here alone I am certainly not misled, he says that the god becomes present to us *in the figure of death*. This I do understand.

The Dagger

I lie atop the escritoire. I look down and decipher her words, since they are upside down to me, those words that are rising off the green paper—green to soothe her reddened eyes. I read of Mora and Musa and Nadira, her brave masks. I make no critical jabs, I do not carve and dissect. I merely report what I am reading.

—I am Mora, she cries, the daughter of Torlat and the beloved of a Scandinavian king of yesteryear! And I will die in battle for the king; I will die as the king sleeps in his tent. I will be what Patroclus was for Achilles. I will take up the sword and do battle against Karmor the Warrior. Of course I will suffer defeat at Karmor's mighty hand: I was born with the temerity of a man and the biceps of a woman.

She grasps the sword that she can scarcely lift and fights in the stead of somnolent royalty. The result is quick and bloody.

Why does she do it? She yearns for the great deed, the deed that reflects the heroic excellence of those who stand at the forefront in a losing battle, the staggering act that everyone says is beyond a woman's power and place. She would occupy that place, never mind the biceps. She will die for love if she cannot live for it, and the bards, perched on her gravemound, will sing her renown.

—Lay on! she shouts. I thirst for battle! In the face of danger my courage jubilates. Lay on!

I will spare you the scene of her slaughter—*pierced through is her white breast, her jet locks are swimming in blood*—but not the rhapsodies of the bards and the lament of the king, belatedly wakened by the battle cries, her own cry a lilting soprano.

—Sing, you bards, sing the praise of the lovely daughter of Torlat! Sing the maiden's praise so that her beauty, withering so soon, may blossom undyingly.

And sing they do.

—Mora, you have fallen with all your beauty, you have collapsed in your very blossoming. You roaring mountain stream leaping from the peaks and foaming waves and tumultuous winds, you howl over the plain, but no mountain stream or wave or storm will waken Mora! Mora, flowering springtime will not rouse you, nor the glistening morn nor the purple eventide, nor the love call. It is splendid to wander in the light of life, but the tomb is narrow and dark. Eternal is the slumber. Therefore, weep for Mora, for she will never recur, she will never come to light again.

Karoline

I assisted more than one sister in their dying. The most terrible death for me was Charlotte's. Of all the women in the family she was the one with intelligence and grace and verve—and because of the intelligence, the wit and verve never descended into silliness. She was our artist, our Leonardo, but also our art critic. When I was nineteen I had my portrait painted in profile. Charlotte congratulated me on my vanity: she said that the portrait was so horrid—it gave me an uglier nose than any nose nature had ever planted on a face—that she knew I had commissioned it so that all my friends would exclaim how little justice it did me. Charlotte! At age sixteen! And how graceful she was. She was our dancer. Her feet barely touched the earth.

And then suddenly she was bedridden and going gaunt, panting for breath, paler each day than the last, her flesh diminishing, moldering, as though already in the grave. The blood she coughed up was red only because of the contrast with her blanched skin. Her once laughing lips became wan lines drawn about a groaning mouth; her cheeks sank, the cheekbones jutted; her beautiful nose drooped, her teeth protruded, imitating the death mask to come. She was a wounded animal, a feral catastrophe. I prayed it would end, prayed she would die quickly. I wanted her back, but not like this, not as a ruin, a cadaver gasping for the oxygen that was killing her as it killed my sweet Novalis.

Too many contradictions, too many confusions in this glorious and wretched life of ours. After she died, I dreamed of her. I was walking at her side through a lovely landscape. Facing us was a small cottage in ruins, surrounded by grain fields and pasture land. But all the ears of grain were drooping to the ground, as though unable to support their own weight. Lotte was dressed in white. She was pallid, unsteady on her feet. My soul was already in mourning.

—Times change, I said to her, and they change so suddenly. Generations pass away, and you are so sick, you too will soon pass away.

—Ah! she cried. Don't be sad that the generations pass away and that I too will soon pass away.——

That was the end of the dream. Those two hiatuses are all I can believe in now.

Do I not believe in immortality, then? Of course I do, of course I believe in immortality. I have to.

The Dagger

The song for Mora fades as the page turns. The song of Musa rises now off a new page, the muse who sings her own unflagging desire for death.

—Come! Kill me! I shall fall, as falling becomes me, clad in purple, kingly, lordly! This death is worth my life—so come!

Musa's brave challenge fades as the page turns again. And now Nadira, the splendid songstress, approaches her own king. Nadira, songstress of sweet melancholy! Jet locks flow over your brow, Nadira, like thoughts of mourning, glistening tears extinguish the fire in your eyes, your voice hovers softly over the thrum of your lyre's strings as softly as spring breezes hover about fragrant blooms, and now you sing!

The spirit of the dead man rises as an apparition. His ghost is covered in blood, but the specter's words to the man who slew him are words of forgiveness.

—The dried blood on your dagger is guiltless, the final words of my death rattle were words of forgiveness.

With that, the bloody apparition sinks back into the sea. Waves splash. Their wash covers entirely the blood-clotted locks.

As the apparition sinks into the sea, the page turns once again, and a youth visits the fresh grave of his defunct beloved. Elves enter on the scene. They cut a caper on the girl's gravemound. The youth joins their dance, which only seems a desecration. Theirs is a danse macabre, since the love tie that bound them is now a bond of death. The youth sings:

For I share my life with shades beneath the earth;
Thirstily they suck from me the juices of my youth.

I know the refrain of these pages now by heart. Mora, Musa, Nadira, and the youth who loves and dances the death dance, they are all singing it. She sings it over and over again behind a dozen masks, and the masks do not muffle her voice. They magnify it.

The paths descend, dark and deep,
Into the shady mortal keep

Where dwells tranquility,
Where hues of life all fade,
The elements are gainsaid,
And peace has firm stability.
Those about me mourn with me,
Out pours my life in all its pain
Like drops of dew dissolving in the sea.
Universal now is mourning's reign.
And so, come! I feel my force is waning,
My thoughts dissolve in dreams.
The pale embers not sustaining,
Existence naught but pain, it seems.

It sounds uncanny, I know, coming from so young and fragile a creature—all this heroic literature, all this knightly bravado and medieval melancholy. But I once heard her confessing the cause of it to a friend, and ever so slowly, as I read her letter, I am beginning to understand.

—It is an ugly fault of mine that I can so readily fall into a state of torpor, and I am happy about every occasion that tears me out of such a state. Yesterday I read Ossian's *Darthula*, and it had such a pleasant effect on me. The old wish to die a hero's death seized me most intensely. It seemed unbearable to me that I should live on, unbearable that I should die a peaceful death, a common sort of death. I often had the very unwomanly wish to throw myself into the tumult of savage battle and to die. Why wasn't I a man! I hold no truck with womanly virtues, have nothing to do with womanly contentment. I enjoy only the wild, the magnificent, the grandiose. It comes from a dire but incorrigible imbalance in my soul; it will remain like this, it has to, for I am a woman, and I have the cravings of a man—without a man's strength. That is why I am so erratic, so much at sixes and sevens with myself.

II

Karoline

Savigny and I were finally alone that evening out on the balcony. It had been a beautiful day, with a lot of happy chatter, but so many people were crowding us—the situation was impossible. I had already written my friends about him. From the start I had been drawn to the gentle dolor that seemed to flow from the very core of him: himself an orphan, he seemed to me a brother. Before long that draw became a secret longing in me, a kind of languor that found me reaching for him or being stretched out by him. Finally, I realized that my languishing betrayed a passion. My friends warned me that I had too little to offer him, he was too good-looking, of such sterling character, and from such a wealthy family, was I not reaching too high? I considered whether I did not need a new circle of friends. But I knew they were right. I felt all too strongly how remote I was from the high ideals he held when it came to women, felt that I had no right to hope, that I shouldn't even dream, that for him I would always be naught, nugatory, subnumerary. For me, he would have to remain the mere shadow of a dream.

Yet there we were, the two of us, out on the balcony and finally alone, wisteria climbing up the wall beneath us and bathing us both in its scent. He said he could see that we were going to be friends. I said that we were already brother and sister and that we would always be close. We would be family. He said yes we would be, yes we already were. We kissed. His mouth was fresh and sweet. My insides went molten. I waited for him to release the words that were pressing against his lips, begging to come out. But my own words about our being brother and sister must have confused him.

—So, how is your brother doing?

—Sorry?

—Your brother. Hector. How's he doing?

—Hector is well, I believe.

I could have smacked him. At a moment like that he asks me about my brother?! I should have slapped him silly so he would see how mad I was at him. And about him.

I thought of another sketch I had drawn for my story about the nymph Calypso. After Odysseus abandons her, his son Telemachos comes to her island in search of his father. Calypso now falls in love with the son as well—he is the very image of his father. But Telemachos' tutor Mentor admonishes the boy to avoid Calypso's clutches, and Mentor and pupil both escape from the island. They have already embarked when Calypso rushes to the shore. In my drawing, their boat is departing, and Calypso throws gravel and stones at them. It looks as though she is throwing them her garter, but it is actually a rock or two. Savigny was lucky there was no gravel on the balcony.

Some time later, I was seeing him off, and I accidentally slammed the coach door on his hand. For years after that, long after he had married Gunda Brentano, a woman who unlike her siblings had no ideas and no relation to the ideal, no real feeling for anything in the universe, a woman to whom the Graces too had been ungenerous, he would say that his hand still hurt, that the pain was recurrent, and that he would never forgive me. That made me very happy, and only afterward very ashamed.

Savigny

It is time that I marry. The only question is who. But whoever it may be, I do have to marry and start a family. Why? Because without the family there is no civil society, without civil society no state, and without a state no law and no jurists. And so I must marry, my advancement depends on it. Only two options, as far as I can see, in spite of my rather large circle of acquaintances: either Günderrode or Gunda—the names almost seem to rhyme, or the first seems to be an expansion of the second, even though the two of them are night and day.

What are the decisive categories pertaining to such a decision? I must think lucidly. Quality of family, dowry, personality, health, romance, in no particular order, even though the proper ordering of the categories decides everything. Let me try to draw up a balance sheet, as though preparing a brief for litigation, where argument and counterargument are crucial to the eventual judgment. Let me try, although this is offensive to me: it contradicts my poetic sensibility. Yet there is no way around the need for a decision, so let me begin.

Gunda

Quality of family. In spite of the Italian background, exceptional, one of the first families of Frankfurt. Not of the old nobility, at least not north of the Alps, but with the powerful influence that comes of wealth. The Brentano children are all gifted—in trade and finance or in music and poetry, especially Clemens and Bettine, both gifted writers.

Günderrode

Quality of Family. Günderrode's father's background is similar to that of my own father; her mother flighty, of no consequence. After her father's early death, financial difficulties, the family now impoverished, albeit not entirely destitute. The children all gifted, but three of K's sisters died too young to show what they might have been capable of.

Health. Gunda, like most of her brothers and sisters, seems to be basically healthy, likely to have sturdy offspring. This is important because of the disasters in my own family, to wit, the early demise of parents and siblings.

Personality. Steady, reliable. No surprises. Basic domestic skills. She will make a trustworthy wife. Not interested in ideas. Tendency to irony, occasional sarcasm, otherwise fine. Clearly devoted to me.

Romance. Not a great deal of imagination, rather prosaic, although quite self-confident and with a biting sense of humor. I have no real experience of her, not yet at any rate, but I believe I can bring myself to love her.

Dowry. The family has been doing exceedingly well for many generations now and owns multiple properties. Gunda is the oldest girl in the family.

Health. Karoline's health too is dubious. She is perhaps consumptive, talks of chest pains, complains often about migraine. Eye problems. Problematic when it comes to producing healthy progeny—given my own family history.

Personality. Shy to diffident. Uncertain of her own excellence. Voracious reader, even of philosophy. Interested in everything. Poet. High ideals, demands impossibly much of herself, perhaps also of others.

Romance. Drawn to her from the beginning. Her eyes, pure cobalt, give me no rest. Her form graceful. Marvelous hands. Even if we do not marry, cannot marry, I will keep her in my life, one way or another. The stuff of dreams.

Dowry.——

Trages

I, the Savigny summer estate, should by rights have been hers as well as his, my wrought iron gate locking out the rest of the world but opening its arms to her, all the rooms of my central residence available to her, along with the stable of horses, the carriages and sleighs, the hedges and fountains—all of it hers, if only he had possessed a heart in his breast, a head on his shoulders, and a brain in that head. She would have been the one sauntering by the magnolia trees beyond the gate and drifting gracefully down the gravel path past the guardhouse and up the double set of red sandstone stairs to the bubbling fountain that graces the approach to the villa's main entrance. Hers would have been the grand trees that tower over the grounds, hers the flower gardens with blooms of every description and exotic scent, hers the outlying buildings, including the redbrick lodge that houses her now behind its oaken door and silver handle, the lodge to which she is reduced, safe, to be sure, from the predations of Clemens but otherwise an all-too-modest domicile for a woman of her stature, albeit infinitely better than the Residence in Frankfurt to which she is normally confined with matrons twice her age and half her wit, but still far too modest, too plain, too simple a residence for such a one. She should have had the lodge and the big house too with its two stories of countless windows and balconies and its three-storied towers at both ends, its ballroom and chandeliers, its kitchen and pantries, its wine cellar and storage spaces, the big house with its personnel in livery, maids to dress and undress her, butlers to serve the tea and sumptuous, nourishing meals, the sandy alleyways for afternoon boule or Provençal pétanque, the lush emerald lawn for evening croquet.

Yet here she is in the April of her lifetime forced to observe and pretend to bless Savigny as he makes this terrible miscalculation. The master of the house has made his choice, and it is a woeful blunder! It is as though he is punishing himself and hurting his estate, verily spiting Paradise, and for what? It seems unnatural! Am I really expected to celebrate the nuptials of what silly Bettine calls these two Birds of Paradise, the new Adam and Eve, to wit, Savigny and Gunda? I see myself delivered over to the hands of the wrong woman, and this is not good.

Everything that was created was seen to be good, says Scripture, but why was this not so with human beings? Why ought they to be and to do otherwise than they are and do? It is lamentable! This question, itself an insight, inspires in me a melancholic meditation. To slaughter one's sensibilities and desires on the sacrificial altar of Necessity—this is what humans call virtue. Virtue is thus killing oneself piecemeal. To stand triumphantly over the ruins of one's own spirit and to proclaim, *See here at my feet the vanquished, the manacled, and all that have been burned at the stake—my will is victorious over them all!* What madness! Yet this is the reward that the virtuous claim for themselves. Vainglorious triumph! For my part, I mourn the manacled and the murdered, the victims of "virtue," and I demand of the self-proclaimed victor: Why? why have you done this?

Karoline

Savigny had enchanted me right from the start, and I never got over the infatuation. His very presence worked magic—a magic that was hazardous for sensitive souls since, like a clever coquette, he sent out amiable looks in all directions, and each soul secretly believed that he or she was the sole intended recipient. I was certain that I was the one, however undeserving.

We exchanged letters over the years, but his were either formal and forced or flirtatious and flip. Especially after his marriage, when he and Gunda would write me together, the letters were unbearable. *O Petite Günderrode, you are a silly little Günderrode, we love you because you are our sheepish little lamb, you silly Günderrode.* At one point I asked him not to write me anymore: he was only writing either because he knew he had disappointed me or because he wanted something from me that I could never give him. He replied that my letters showed signs of disorder. I answered that my head lacked several organs, among them the organ for order, but I did not fail to add that he too was lacking in some respects. For example, how could such a learned man have learned so little about love? That head full of proud knowledge clearly still had plenty of room for delusion.

Our correspondence dwindled after that, but it did not end. It became a ring-around-a-rosy of misunderstandings among the three of us, Gunda, me, their "Petite Günderrode," and Savigny himself—Gunda full of irony about my creative work, asking me how I could be so enthusiastic over what exhibited so little talent, and Savigny trying to negotiate between the warring G's of his life. I told him how furious I was over our little balcony scene, that I would never forgive him, and he confessed his clumsiness and his sometime love, but he added that his hand still hurt, and had I not done it on purpose? I told him about Gunda's ironizing and condescension, about her conviction that my dissatisfaction with her derived from the fact that I could not bear her having the upper hand, since Savigny was hers and not mine, and still Savigny—ever the jurist—tried to work out a settlement between us. It is a flaw in me, I know it and I hate it, but I do not settle. I accept no consolation prizes.

When Savigny and Gunda married in April 1804 and we were all at Trages, I decided I owed him a wedding present, something for him alone. I sent him a little sonnet. I do not see how I could have been more candid.

41

The Dream Kiss

A kiss breathed life into my unrest,
Nursed the deep wound within my breast.
Darkness, come! embrace me on this wedding night,
That these lips of mine may suck a new delight.
My life was dipped this way into the stream,
That I might live to dream eternally the dream.
I now despise all other joys that I might have,
Since night alone exudes so sweet a salve.
The day is spare with sweet delights of love
The idle boasts of sunlight do but pain me
And embers of light from hence can only scorch me.
So shield yourself, my eye, from glaring earthly suns
Submerge yourself in night. Night will nurture your desire
And cooling waters born of Lethe quell the burning fire.

Such was the imperfectly rhymed dream kiss delivered by Savigny's Petite Günderrode on his (not her) wedding day, a kiss for someone who was dear to me from someone who, alas, will love him forever. As on that day of wisteria and gravel.

O Savigny, Savigny! I am inclined to perceive in you a certain injustice with regard to my innermost nature, and to that extent my confidence in you has a clearly demarcated limit. If you are angry with me, then it is very unjust of you, for I have been such a good girl all this while.

Bettine

Eventually I did learn how to philosophize, at least when our beds were right up against each other, and once the lamp was out we could talk through the night. Interrupted only by the wind rattling the roof or the mice bustling behind the walls, our talk would solve all the problems of the universe. Ours were grand speculations, profoundest thoughts, sentiments so deep, so weighty, that the world creaked on its hinges—maybe our thoughts were urging the Earth's very rotation on its axis of love—and I called her my Plato and she called me her Dion of Syracuse. In other words, I was her tyrant, and we pledged to love one another tenderly and give up our lives for the other if need be. But we ruled out suicide. She had read somewhere, in Hemsterhuis, I think, that the *will* to annihilate oneself occurs within time, whereas the *consequences* of such a will are eternal. The very thought of suicide therefore collapses in on itself, annihilates itself, because it is a passing thought; it cloaks itself in eternity, but it is in fact a child of time, indeed the offspring of an evil time. Like every act of will it is a child of *uncaring* time. A veritable visible appearance of the eternal spirit it is not, whereas a human life *is* such an appearance, so that no act of will dare destroy a life. That would be like a slave rebelling against its master.

We did not pause to think that the slave might justifiably rebel, encouraged by all those enlightening and liberating thoughts that were blowing in from France during those years. We did not pause to think that uncaring time itself would stretch on and on in such a way that one might mistake it for the eternally unchanging unpropitious. No, there would be no such mistake, no swan song from either of us, that was all there was to it. Even in my own bed, wrapped in my own featherbed, I could feel her warmth.

—Good night, my sweet swan, my dear Plato, let us find Hypnos on the altar of Eros.

sappho

what is the most splendid sight on earth? some say a cavalry of riders storming by or a throng out on parade, some say a fleet of sailing ships is the most luminous sight in this dark world, but i say it is the sight of someone you are bound to love and this is not hard to prove since helen, who outshone all others in beauty, was led astray by a single glimpse of paris and abandoned a perfectly good husband and headed straight for troy without a thought to her daughter or her parents. as for me i remember a girl named anaktoria her graceful gait and that flickering light on her cheek which i would rather see again in times to come than all the chariots of lydia or your navies or your host of horsemen. when i first saw her, love shook my heart as a blast of wind shakes a mountain oak. she alas was taken with a godlike man who sat across from her close enough to sip the sweetness of her voice, but i was taken with her golden glittering laughter and i sent her the thoughts that were searing my mind—

when i see you even for an instant my voice cracks my tongue freezes a low fire rages beneath my skin. blinded by lightning bolts stunned by bursts of thunder in my ears i am shivering with sweat as chills tremors quakes afflict me and i turn the color of parched grass and in a moment i think i will be dead. you burn me. i remember all the things we used to do. you came and i was mad for you and you cooled my mind but left the rest of me aflame. the one i care for most is most careless of me and does me the most harm. and now once again this eros this loosener of limbs this bittersweet eros troubles my own limbs. but you who came from heaven wrapped in a porphyry cloak of all the stars the brightest you have forgotten me. i prayed to aphrodite in a fever dream and now ineluctable love fills me floods me whelms me throttles my being you torture me you plague me like no other and now like a child a helpless infant i cry out for my mother.

Bettine

Oh, Karoline! You were standing so close to me on that dreary November evening as we looked out onto the garden. You were very quiet, absorbed in the twilight. Finally you spoke to me the words that were about to come out of my own mouth.

—Why are you so quiet today?

—I know I'm a chatterbox. But I'm preoccupied today. And you?

A long pause.

—Sometimes my soul goes mute. Everything inside seems dead.

—That's how it is with you now? Dead?

—Everything inside me resembles everything out there in the garden, lost in twilight. The dark comes over my soul as it does over those bushes. They lose their color, they sense that they've lost it, but even so it *is* lost.

I did not reply, did not dare to say any more. I drifted over to the window seat and lay down on my back and closed my eyes. Time passed. You lit a lamp. I could see the light through my eyelids and my tears. When I opened my eyes you were standing over me. You bent over as though to study me closely. You saw the look on my face and you tried to explain.

—I often feel something like a hole in my chest, a gap, a vacancy. I can't touch it. It is nothing, but it hurts.

—Can't I fill it?

—That too would hurt.

I touched your face with my hand, got up, swung my cloak about my shoulders, and left. Your eyes were on me as I walked out the door.

On the way home I wrapped my arms around myself. I imagined I was carrying you to a safe place at the end of the earth. I loved you so much! I dreamed I would settle you down on a bed of moss and serve you and allow nothing that might hurt you to touch you. I thought for a moment I could do this for you, even though I knew I could not. I was like a child who mixes up the near and the far, thinking she can grasp the moon, fetch it down out of the night sky and give it to a friend who needs it.

Clemens Brentano

My sister Bettine is dear to me, far dearer than dreary Gunda, but how dizzy she is, how scatterbrained and unfocused! It must run in the family. In me it is excused by genius; she has no such alibi. I have to explain things to her as though I were her father, since our own father could explain nothing and brother Franz is a dullard, leaving me to give her the proper counsel that every girl needs as she comes of age.

I fear the influence Günderrode is having on her. If Bettine needs a poet as a model for her own future, I am that poet, not a woman possessed of a masculine mind, a woman who cannot feel as a woman must feel. The sublime seriousness, the depth of meaning, the earnestness of purpose were all evident in the Günderrode poems that Bettine sent me. But why did not Karoline herself send them to me? I would have helped her. I would have edited her, improved her. She disdained my help. And then she dared to *publish* the sorts of things no woman has ever written or ever should write. As for publishing in general, I am often sad when I see a new author appearing in print, for it is proof that he no longer has any friends and so has had to appeal to an indifferent public. But that is by the bye.

Bettine, dear, listen to me. I have already explained these things to our Gunda and now I have to explain them to you. Everything you do—all you women, without exception—must be either utterly charming or have to do with the caretaking of another person; it must engage you on the sole basis of your single purpose in life, which is to lure us men away from our service to the state so that at any given moment you can lead us back to naked life and in this way become mothers. Otherwise how can I account for that mysterious aura that arouses pleasure and even devotion in me, the aura that surrounds every blossoming breedable virgin; how, unless it be the sheer transparency that gazes back at me eternally as the production of our eternally enduring humankind? And everything is holy which, while remote from us, is yet our own; everything becomes holy when we touch it and seize it bodily. It is Creation, which proceeds by way of pleasure alone. The so-called great deeds of a woman have always seemed to me utterly fatal unless they are compelled by the sex drive or the maternal instinct. A woman can never be a "great" human being without her betraying to me the secret of her disgusting infertility.

The Dagger

She thumbs through the pages of her *Poems and Fantasies*, her first book, perched proudly on her lap. I am nestled comfortably on the armrest of the upholstered chair, and I read along with her. All those mystifying Celtic names, the names that fraudulent Ossian gave her and that sent her imagination soaring. She could do whatever she wanted with them. Darthula, Erin's most beautiful maiden, foremost among the young Hibernian women, as courageous as Joan of Arc! How exalted the writer felt when she let that enemy arrow fly, the arrow that Darthula's shield could not stop! Darthula sinks like a column of pure snow in the sun, her dark locks spreading luxuriantly over the ground where she falls. She sleeps the endless sleep. Her beauty will never shine forth again.

And Thia, whose name echoes her own nom de plume and who avenges her father's murder—by killing her own lover. She would prefer to plunge a dagger into her lover's breast while he is making love to her, but she has to settle for a shared plunge into the sea. Dressed all in black, Thia leads Timur to the very precipice from which he threw her beloved father into the abyss—that had been sweet revenge for Timur, but now it is Thia's turn. She had loved him so intensely! But now she flings back her veil and reveals herself to him. Timur must have a sudden premonition of his doom, but he is overcome by love. He reaches out to her. Before he realizes what is happening, she throws her arms around his neck and tosses him—tosses them both—into the raging surf. Their bodies shatter on the rocks below, their blood flows together in a scarlet embrace of love and vengeance, and the surging tide of the sea covers them in its veil of mist. Turn the page.

Karoline's Don Juan enters at stage left. Her poem is something completely new, no longer the usual moralizing complaint by a woman against a profligate and inconstant lover. For she makes the Don—and not the wronged woman—her hero. Don Juan burns with love for another's bride, whom by holy law he may never touch. Yet the flame of his yearning burns hotter than any hell to which the good burghers would condemn him. He goes to her, risks everything, knowing that she is thinking only of him.

A murderer's dagger strikes his breast,
With joy he goes to join the dead.

Sweet memory will take him to his rest,
Recalling to him that loveliest hour when
Her mouth found his in the palace tower,
Her arms the answer to his quest.

Whenever it is a matter of fidelity or fickleness, of being true or faithless, the author joins forces with Don Juan and, turning the page, with Narcissus too. Violetta cries, *You are not true!* and Narcissus replies, *To beauty alone am I faithful, I change when change I must.* Violetta cries, *Is there no love that can compel you?* and Narcissus retorts with words from the writer's own mouth:

The hours turn in rounds eternal,
The stars will drift without abode,
The brook will hasten from its source
    and not look back;
The stream of life will swell
    and then fall back
And tear me along in its mighty surge.
Behold all life! naught will last,
Eternal wand'ring till all is past.
Change is life, a motley vital striving!
Oh, stream, to you I commit my living!
Forget the land, embrace the surge!
To you, to you, all urge and urge!

On every page the mouth of that slender woman's body opens and releases the voice of a man. That pale hand moves across the page and leaves manly traces. An absurd creature, this Tian. Were anyone to read her they would be baffled. Were anyone to ask me to explain I would grow taciturn.

But now she moves to her secretary and writes a letter to a friend. She takes me with her. I peer from above and I decipher what she writes. I am beginning to understand more deeply—perhaps because of the published book—what I mean to her.

—You will certainly have felt this simple phenomenon in you, when tragic moments pass through you and conjure up in you an image from history, and when all the circumstances surrounding this image or figure form a chain that causes you to feel profound pain or elevated sublimity: you battle against injustice, you are victorious, you are happy, everything tends to go your way, you develop forces in yourself that become mighty, you are able to stretch your spirit in such a way that it extends over all things; or, by contrast, a hard fate confronts you, you bear it, matters become increasingly galling, they ravage even those consecrated spaces of your bosom, your fidelity and love; your tutelary spirit takes you by the hand and leads you out of the country that endangered your elevated ethical worth, and the call of that spirit makes you soar; under his protection you may hope to escape further suffering, so that you strike out in the direction commanded by an inner spirit of sacrifice.—Such appearances are what spirit, by way of fantasy, experiences as destiny; spirit tests itself there, and it is certain that spirit often internalizes experiences of heroism in that way; one feels permeated by the sublime, by things one would perhaps be too weak to withstand were one to confront them in the flesh. But fantasy is the place where the seed is planted and the plant takes root, and who knows when or how it will blossom as a mighty and pristine force in oneself?—How else will the hero in us ever come to stand?—No such workshop of spirit exists in vain, and however that force may come to act on the outside world, its essential vocation is surely to work on our inner life.—And so I feel a kind of calming effect come over me when I look at my very slight and quite inconspicuous literary creations. For they are the footsteps of my spirit, and I do not renounce them. Even if someone should object that I ought to have waited until riper and tastier fruits were there for the harvesting, it was my own conscience that urged me to accept them and not to reject them, not any of them, since if a creature of mine should ever come to be that walks and talks and is truly alive, it will pertain to that entire process, and all that I have undergone in this fashion up to now will prove to be what has brought me here to this point where stands my unshakable will.

Friedrich Creuzer

I first met her at friend Daub's house. Daub and his wife were childhood companions of hers. I was looking out the window into the splendid late-summer garden and I was thinking of Persia. It was the fourth of August 1804, a date incised forever in my memory. She came up noiselessly behind me. I sensed her presence more than heard it; I turned and met the eyes of Pallas Athena. She was my height. Our eyes met on the same level, as did our minds. I told her what I was working on. She nodded, as if she understood. Unable to believe it, I tested her.

—Not merely the old Persian religion of Zarduscht that we always read about, I said, but the possible role of Zeruane Akherene in that religion.

Her eyebrows rose. Her mouth worked in the way I would come to know well. It endeared her to me immediately.

—That's a name I've never heard before, she said.

I offered a brief explanation of the mother of all numbers, not herself a number but the mother of all ciphers, a valiant explanation from a man who had just then been struck by lightning. Later our talk became easier, more familiar, but I cannot remember a word of what we may have said.

Two days later came the picnic at Neuburg. By the end of that day I knew that my former life had ended, that everything now depended on her. I had been married for five years by then, and my life had settled into a dependable routine. A great deal of work got done, I have to admit. Leske had been my professor. I carried his satchel of books to the lecture hall in the morning, I brought him his coffee in the afternoon, and so it seemed natural that after his death I should carry the burdens of his professorship and his widow. Their son and daughter were only half grown, and they needed a father. I needed the domestic comforts. Besides, I was in debt to Savigny, and Sophie's small pension and healthy inheritance would help me to acquit that debt. Savigny himself encouraged the marriage, but not on account of the debt, money meant nothing to him, or next to nothing, he was born into it.

Sophie was thirteen years older than I, so that I did not expect her to make demands on me. I was able through cautious diplomacy to reduce those demands to a minimum, but when they intensified I could barely suppress my nausea. By that time in my life I had given up on Eros except as a topic of research. Eros was the child of Poverty and Plenty, conceived at the time of Aphrodite's birth. Now, Aphrodite is beauty, and beauty had been bestowed on others but on neither Sophie nor me, and I had adjusted my expectations.

Karoline readjusted those expectations in the way a lightning bolt readjusts a tree. Not long after the picnic, perhaps some days later, that same small company visited the castle. We were up on the ramparts, atop a turret of some kind. She signaled to me. She wanted to show me something down below, the bridge over the river, a passing barge, a fishing boat, I do not know, something about the river. I saw only her delicate hand. She turned to me. Her eyes said infinitely more than her words and gestures, however, and ever since that moment the castle turret is my domicile and the center of my existence.

And so I wrote the cousin with whom I have shared the few stirring moments of my life, the man who alone understands the depths of my loneliness.

—My heart overflows the banks of time and swells to infinity. . . . You should know that I find myself in heaven. She has given me a pendant, a sensuous symbol that I wear now over my heart. The die is cast—there is no way out, no possible compromise—it is heaven or death. Let the tragedy commence.—I am on my way to steal some good-night kisses.—Think well on what I here confide to you.

Clemens Brentano

Our firstborn had died of scarlet fever that May. All of life changed on that day of death. Everything. Mereau and I could bear Marburg no longer; we moved south to Heidelberg. We would make a new start. It was late summer 1804. Mereau was in Frankfurt trying to get to know my impossible family. I stayed in Heidelberg.

A friend from the university, Daub, invited me to come along on a picnic that a group of his colleagues were planning. I was in no mood. When I learned that Günderrode would be among them, however, I said yes. I brought along my zither, knowing that my folk songs and my playing would soften her heart toward me, if anything would. That was always my best play, my best ploy, with the women. Never good enough, alas, but even so, it was my chance. We survive by trying.

All were settled comfortably on blankets in a copse of the wood near the Neuburg Institute. All ate delicate sandwiches. All drank mildly fermented apple juice. I sang. Günderrode, all in white, was sitting close to an unprepossessing scrawny little man I had met before in Marburg but did not know very well. Later I learned to appreciate his research on the religions and legends of sundry ancient peoples, but on that day he seemed to me a pitiful specimen. Except for the way Günderrode glanced at him and he at her. It infuriated me. I almost jumbled the lyrics, not that anyone would have noticed.

Lovers are so naïve, so bemused. They think they are acting so discreetly that no one would ever guess. They are as discreet as a St. John's fire on a hilltop, a wheel of straw all ablaze and bounding down the mountainside, qualms of smoke and leaping tongues of flame visible for miles. That's why their friends always notice it before they do.

—Oh, but at that point I wasn't sure yet, they protest.

—Ah, but I was entirely sure, I reply.

I was incensed. The songbird and the scarecrow? It could not be. And yet clearly it was. Smoke and fire everywhere. I searched my mind for a fitting encore, one that might accompany my dismal discovery, a *Princess and the Frog* sort of song, but I could think of none. I stopped singing. All applauded nicely. I drank some more apple juice.

Karoline

Melete to Eusebio: I often think back with joy to the day we first found one another, when I approached you in helpless reverence, as a catechumen hungry for instruction approaches a high priest. I was determined to please you in whatever way possible, and the consciousness of my own worth would have been shattered altogether if you had turned away from me in indifference. I still do not understand how I was able to win you over to such a degree; my own tutelary spirit must have been doing double duty for me during that first conversation. A new life opened for me then and there. For in you alone do I feel that I have been elevated to those supreme insights in which everything profane has gone up in smoke like an absurd dream. That elevation became my prevailing state of mind; in you the supernal ideas have become reality for me here on Earth. The rest of us mortals have to fast, preparing ourselves bodily and spiritually when we go to sup with the Lord; you receive the god daily without having to undertake such preparations.

To me, O friend, the heavenly powers are not so propitious, and I am often heavy of heart, on what account I am not exactly sure, whether myself or our times, inasmuch as our age is so impoverished when it comes to inspiring enthusiasm for artists of any kind. Everything grand and overpowering has been dispersed among the infinite mass of us, so that it dwindles to almost nothing. A wretched justice is our destiny! In order that no one be sated and no one starve, we all have to make do with sober destitution. Is it any wonder such "economizing" in all things and in every sense of that word has become for us all such a significant virtue?

The squalor of our life—let us admit it—coincides with the rise of Protestantism. Everyone has access to the chalice now, the layman as well as the anointed priest, so that no one imbibes sufficient to be full of God, and those few drops that each receives satisfy no one. Not a soul realizes what they are missing, however, and so everyone is merely swallowed up in disputation and protest.

Eusebio to Melete: Only what we are able to survey from a distance can assume a proper shape for us. Our own times press on us so closely that we are like embryos in the mother's womb. Can we say anything meaningful about our times? We observe particular symptoms, and now and then we take the pulse of our century, inclined as we are to conclude that it is sick. But every individual thing is part of an abyssal network; it is a night in which universal concepts can shed only the faintest light on things. Therefore, my friend, because we can descry only a few patterns in that immense tapestry which the spirit of the Earth is weaving as our own times, let us be modest. There is a sort of devotion in which alone we can find happiness, completeness, and peace, a way of looking at things which I might call absorption in the divine. Let us try to achieve that, and not go about lamenting the fate of the universe. In order that you may see more clearly what I mean by this, I am sending you some books on Hindu religion.

Melete to Eusebio: Because I cannot extend my reach beyond the limits of our own times, do you not think it would be more advisable for me to abandon the path of my own poetic productions and undertake serious study of the poets of earlier times, especially those of the Middle Ages? I realize of course that such study would require a great deal of work. And I would have to amputate a limb from my own natural being. For I am happiest when I look upon the productions of my spirit, and it is only in some creation or other that I am able to attain true consciousness of my self. But to achieve one thing, I know, one must be prepared to sacrifice something else—that is a universal fate, and it should not disarm me.

Eusebio to Melete: The vision of the path you must take lies clearly before me, best beloved, since from the very first moment you approached me I recognized who you were. Your path will always remain in my consciousness as having been ordained by God. Never have I seen a human being's face for the first time in such a way; never have I heard a human voice that was accompanied by such a feeling; and this godlike quality, this stamp of Necessity, has always pervaded my thoughts of you. And so I also know what is necessary in you and for you; I recognize the entire way you must live in nature, in poesy, and in divine wisdom. I know therefore that it is not fitting to prescribe such oppressive studies to and for *you*. To be sure, the great artistic masters of earlier times are there to be read and understood, but if it is a question of *schools* of art, then I say that those masters belong to *what has been*, and therefore we should not expect that they may be born once again. Infinite nature always wants to reveal itself anew over an infinite time. In the fullness of the centuries, Brahma has appeared many times, but always in novel transformations. Never has he assumed the identical shape. Thus everyone should engage himself and create in the manner he is called upon to do, going where the spirit leads him, not rejecting any of his compositions as dissonant. And so I entertain no doubts about your own case: the force that dwells and strives in such a person will give him no rest. Often the heart will suffer pains and pangs, until the idea, newly born, has stilled the agony and the longing of its gestation.—

Yesterday I experienced several blessed hours on top of the world. I had climbed a hillside on whose slopes every trace of human habitation, every sign of human use and purpose, had vanished. Things were well with me, and I felt quite cheerful. Two splendid herons soared over my head, bathing their carefree breasts in the blue depths of the sky. Ah, I thought, if only a human being might belong in this way to the sky—everything on Earth seemed minuscule to me. In such moments only what is eternal has value, only the creative genius and the holiest heart of hearts. Then I thought of you, as I always do when nature touches me. Many times, at the moment when the last rays of the sun illuminated the river, I have delivered over to its flow my thoughts of you, as though the current would carry those thoughts to you so that they might play about in your head. Fare thee well! In my best hours I am always with you.

Melete to Eusebio: There is still one thing that delivers the most crushing blow to my inmost heart of hearts, and that is the fact that every mountain peak we scale conceals on its farther side the downward-plunging slope. This thought causes the joy I take in all fresh and youthful things to wither; it mixes into the liquor of my life an inexpressible melancholy. Thus every beginning pleases me more than anything I have completed, and nothing touches me so deeply as the reddening hue that spreads across the sky at sunset. Every evening I want to sink into never-ending night, so as not to outlive the evening's demise. Happy is she who is granted death when joy is in full bloom. Happy is she who can quit the table at the feast of life before the candlelight grows dim and the wine loses its verve. Eusebio! If someday the amiable light of your life should be extinguished for me, oh, then be kind and take me with you, the way divine Pollux took his mortal brother; let me accompany you to Orkus and go with you to the immortal gods, for I do not want to live without you. You are the loveliest of all my thoughts and feelings. All the shapes and blossoms of my being wind themselves around you as the labyrinth of arteries winds about the heart, feeding that heart and lending it its ardor.

The Dagger

A second volume arrives, more modest, slim, even slight, *Poetic Fragments*. I slit open the pages. Some of the fragments are impenetrable to me—a hesitant Mohammed, for example, whom I fail to recognize. But I have to love Hildgund, her favorite heroine and my own. Not the usual love story, none of the usual fatty tissue that fills out and plumps up the silliness. She cuts away the lard and leaves us with the red meat of murder.

The plot? Hildgund, a Burgundian princess with a highly unlikely name catches the eye of Attila the Hun during his rampage through Gaul. She agrees to marry him, much to the chagrin of her fiancé Walther. But Hildgund is thinking as Judith once thought—the Judith of Holofernes fame. Hildgund dreams of a magnificent deed, one that will rid Europe of the Scourge of God. It will be *the greatest deed ever performed by a woman*. Holofernes was child's play compared to Attila, who is a far more forbidding groom to dispatch. Hildgund explains to fiancé Walther her lust for the deed:

> How like a lord a man is, he shapes his destiny.
> The measure of his forces alone defines his end.
> A woman's fate, alas! lies not in her own hand!
> She must obey the stringent will of ethicality.
> Can one evade commands of overweening authority?

But this is precisely what Hildgund proposes to do. Once she is shut of Walther, he too unlikely named, she resolves to woo and deceive the odious Hun. Yet the enormity of her deed gives her pause.

> Why hesitate? Is it too monstrous
> For my pallid, timorous lips to utter?
> The name alone terrifies, ha! murder!
> The deed itself is lawful, bold, illustrious.
> The fate of nations slumbers in my breast,
> I will free myself and liberate the rest!
> So banish fear and caution, O my soul,
> The warrior bold achieves the grandest goal.

She tricks the barbarian king's advisors and tweaks the fearsome king's nose as well. She eschews the poisoned cup to which, as legend informs us, Attila actually succumbed; she has a manlier plan, if Judith of old too was a man. She has a worthier weapon. Already her dagger shivers with anticipation, the steel sings, then steadies itself for the sacrificial thrust.

It is the day of their nuptials. The lavish wedding feast is prepared. *Come!* cries the lusty groom, the savage Hun, to his seemingly reluctant bride. And she?

—I obey, my lord! (*aside:*) Ha!
Celebrate, tyrant,
The fleeting hours of this your final day.

Bravo! Her best little drama by far, if I am any judge, marred only by the precipitous end. For we do not see—she does not depict the scene, she averts her eyes and our own, she will not let us watch—the weapon do its work.

Carl Daub

Whoever attacks the holy estate of matrimony, whoever through word *and deed* suborns a marriage subverts the foundation of civilization. Marriage is the beginning and the culminating point alike of every culture. It tames the savage and graces the most cultivated man—who proves his cultivation by unwavering fidelity to his espoused. Marriage must be indissoluble. It brings so much happiness that all particular unhappinesses cannot keep pace with it. One should not even speak of unhappiness; we simply lose patience from to time, and this is a fault. (Though who will not lose patience with a shrew?) If one allows those moments of impatience to subside, however, one discovers by way of vigorous discipline and unwavering fortitude that one is felicitous after all, happy that one has been able to hold out for so long a time. It is such an achievement! All the civilized world acknowledges it!

There can be no adequate grounds for divorce; no sophisms, whether moral or political, can justify it. The mortal condition is so laden with suffering that the mortifications one member of a couple unloads on the other member do not count for much. And the moral condition of a fallen mortality such as ours proscribes all self-pity: probably we deserve all the misery that is heaped on us despite our protestations of innocence (see the Book of Job). In any case, eternity alone can alleviate all that wretchedness. Patience and long-suffering are all that is required, and death is the dream of infinite patience. Bible study and philosophy and marriage all prepare us for it.

My friend Creuzer is about to lose everything on account of a mindless infatuation with some young thing. (And she is charming, so much is true, but then they always are.) He is about to sacrifice his soul. My role will be to rescue him and his miserable marriage from a fate worse than loneliness. I will write the young woman most solicitously. I too have known her since her childhood, and she trusts me implicitly. I shall practice the fine art of dissuasion. She will see that I am right, and she will desist, since he cannot.

Karoline

Your letter, dear Daub, has brought me many hours of the most painful struggle. I have to ask you: Is it not a genuine marriage when two people understand and love one another entirely, when they possess and are possessed by one another, when the innermost and holiest life of the one is ignited and nurtured by the other alone? And if that is indeed a genuine marriage, is it not a sin against nature when a so-called marriage manacles together two agonizing souls who do not satisfy each other's needs and who do not understand and love one another? Is it a marriage at all that consumes the heart of one of the two in insatiable languor? And just because that same one has made a mistake, must he wither and die on account of it? Who among us can inquire into the secret sufferings of a mishandled heart? If such a person does not immediately die of grief, if he does not immediately open an artery, all are complacent and say that things will soon take a turn for the better. But that turn never comes, and the resulting life is worse than death.

Can you really believe that his wife would have been happy if only I had renounced? Truly, it cannot go well for her if she is aware that she is forcing a husband to stay when he desires fervently to get away from her, such that even if she asserts her claim on him she will never possess him. For one can possess only an other who feels love; otherwise she possesses him as a prison possesses the prisoner. And if it is so difficult for her to surrender such possession, she who still can look forward to a happy future with her children from an earlier marriage, must it not break one's heart to see that the only person who is called upon to renounce is the one who is loved and who loves? It has become clear to me that my renunciation would in the end make no one happy; quite the reverse, it would make several people miserable.

If I am sinning, then I want to remain pure at least with respect to him. I forbid myself any other choice. And if hope were really so blasphemous as you suggest, he would not be able to hope. For he has the holiest sensibility, and I cannot even dream of being the excellent human being that he is. To do what brings him joy is for me a virtue, a duty, and a right, and it makes me happy. But to do something that would torture him? That would be an eternal affront: it would cause him gnawing pain, and it would poison heaven for me.

Young Werther

A marvelous cheerfulness has overrun my entire soul, equal to the fragrant spring morning I am enjoying so wholeheartedly! I am alone, savoring my life here in this unfamiliar region, which was made for souls like mine. I am so happy, my friend, so deeply immersed in the feeling of peaceful existence that work on my art is suffering. I could not sketch a thing right now, not a line, and yet I've never been a greater painter than in these moments. When the lovely valley around me releases its warm, moist air, and when the noonday sun rests atop the trees of this impenetrable shady forest of mine, so that only a single ray of light enters the sanctum sanctorum, I sprawl in the tall grass that shoots up alongside the brook and, having grown closer to the earth, I notice a thousand tiny growing things; when I sense, close to my heart, the microscopic world among the leaves of grass, the world of numberless uncanny shapes of worm and insect, I feel the presence of the Almighty who made us all in His image and I feel the birth pangs of the all-loving One who holds us and sustains us in eternal delight.

May 22

When I see that all our hard work serves merely to satisfy our needs, needs which themselves serve no purpose other than to prolong our meager existence, and then when I see that the peace of mind we achieve in all our efforts, at least beyond a certain point, is merely a sort of dreamlike resignation, then I turn inward in search of a world. Every human being builds a world out of his or her own self. And no matter how barricaded we may feel in that world, we preserve the sweet feeling of freedom in our hearts, the feeling that we can walk out of this prison whenever we like.

July 16

When Charlotte plays the pianoforte it is with angelic force, a force of soul and body. Every melody is a body song. Its magic cures what ails me—even at moments when I feel I could put a bullet through my head. The confusion and the gloom disperse, and I can breathe freely again.

August 8

But can you really demand of a wretched person who is gradually dying of an incurable and unstoppable disease that he put a sudden end to his misery with a thrust of the dagger? Does not the illness that is eating away at his forces also consume the courage that might liberate him?

August 12

Oh, you rational people! Passion! Drunkenness! Madness! You stand there so unconcerned, so uninvolved, you ethical people! You scold the drinker, you spurn the insane, you walk on by like a Pharisee thanking his God that you were not made like one of these. Shame on you, you sober ones! Shame on you, you wise ones!

March 16

I often feel that I would like to open an artery. It would grant me freedom forever.

•

December 21

Young Werther and Charlotte are reading his translations of *Ossian* together. The Celtic bard overwhelms them both. *Deep is the sleep of the dead; far below lies their pillow of dust!* Young Werther and Charlotte kiss. She presses his hand to her breast.

But then she tears herself away from him. Trembling, spinning between love and strife, she cries, *Werther, this is the last time. You will never see me again!*

•

After eleven o'clock

Everything around me is still, and my soul is at peace. In the churchyard, far back in the corner that opens onto the fields, loom the linden trees. I will not ask the pious Christians to lie buried in my vicinity.

The clock strikes twelve.

My soul hovers over my coffin.

Karoline

I need Goethe's *Werther* in my vicinity, always close by, always ready to hand, so that I can consult it the way the ladies of the Residence consult their bibles. I can recite chapter and verse. It is my book of edification and enlightenment when it comes to the two most important things—loving and dying. Death is the long sleep that seals all our love and heals all of love's scars; the brevity of life sutures all our deeper wounds. In these two grand deeds, loving and dying, human beings have to be capable of grand passion, and they have to learn how to rise to the rigors of both, for both are *passio*, and both are bloodstained.

Intense Red

You intense red,
Up to the instant I am dead
Let my loving be like you.
May you never fade
Up to the instant I am dead,
You glowing red.
Let my loving be like you.

Intense red of the sun in the Persian mountains and on the Greek coastal plains—where my companions roam. Zarduscht of Persia, striding off grandly to face his death; Heraclitus, sitting on the temple stairs at Ephesus and playing at lots in his mind as the ever-living sun rolls across the sky; Sicilian Empedocles, forever fugitive, hurried and harried in the vortex of Love and Strife. All of them in *passio*, all of them as blood red as the solar disc itself!

Friedrich Creuzer

I do not approve of the expression Old Cow, even when it curls over my own lips. It is the sort of insult Lukian would have hurled—he is so unkind to womankind in general, being in this respect the consummate pagan, utterly remote from the refinements Christianity has brought us. Karoline invented the name Benefactress for her, and that is both more Christian and more just.

And yet, when she comes in the night and demands my service, it is not the word Benefactress that presses against the wall of my teeth and begs to be uttered. The horrors do not end with her sagging body, those devastations produced by gravity and overeating; the horrors have scarcely commenced with those things. For she cannot stop herself from primping and mewing like a coquette, flirting in cretinously sentimental ways in both gesture and word, so that my gorge rises. I have to swallow the bile that mounts in me.

She compels me to betray my honeyed oaths to K, she makes me unfaithful to the only love I have ever known or ever will know. It is an abomination of nature and culture alike. It is a terrible sin against love and life.

It was not always this way. As soon as I was able to tell her about K she acquiesced, albeit under vulgar tears. She had to admit that she had violated nature by depriving me of my youth; she had taken advantage of my inexperience and ugliness. The thirteen years that separated us—an entire generation—meant that we could have no children of our own, so that our marriage was pointless, a caricature, a mockery. Still she insisted on it. I had to acquiesce so that I could ascend to Leske's professorship—of which she was now the gatekeeper. At the beginning she appeared to have no illusions.

But as soon as there was mention of divorce, the only honorable thing to do, so that I could be free to marry as a young man is supposed to be able to marry, the "Benefactress" began to press her claims on me again, her squalid and unspeakable claims. I cower here in a tiny, frigid room in one of the outbuildings and listen for the nauseating sound of hooves crossing the yard to my door.

Karoline

Years ago I wrote a poem called *Wish*. I'd had that wish so many times that I finally wrote it down. When Charlotte lay dying before my eyes, which were growing dim and red-rimmed behind the tears, or when Savigny chose Gunda over me even though he knew it would be the death of his youth, a long slow death by poisoning, and maybe as far back as my father's death, when I watched his coffin being carried down the stairs and I knew that it meant separation forever, that they would never let him out of that long box—it was always the fright of separation that drove my wish. My wish was to be allowed to accompany and be accompanied, not to be abandoned, to keep the memory of something or someone perpetually present to me, never leaving me, no matter what the cost. My deepest fear was that my memory would betray me.

> In the stream of time you will pale in my mind. If only
> I could die with you, as though the sun had already set,
> And all the colors had vanished in the dark of night.

Do I still believe in immortality? Oh, yes. I wrote a drama about her not long ago—for *Immortalita* is a goddess—and I sent it to Bettine, who as usual understood nothing. I placed Immortalita at the lip of a cave that leads to the underworld. Charon's barge transports the shades across the Styx. Hecate hovers on the shore. The goddess Immortalita stands within a serpentine ring of fire, the coiling snake of eternity, Ouroboros biting its own tail. Furious Ouroboros will not release Immortalita until she finds love.

Meanwhile, a beautiful youth, Erodion, has smuggled himself aboard Charon's barge, hiding amid the gibbering shades. Upon arrival, Erodion tells Immortalita that he is the son of Eros and of Eros's mother Aphrodite. Erodion is the love that makes all the generations possible. He is in search of womanly beauty, the beauty of his own maternal line. He knows he will find it in Immortalita alone, in the pleasure of all her lips and at the tips of her breasts.

—I was living the life of a mummy, but you have breathed a soul into me, she tells him.

Hecate commands Erodion to step into the ring of fire, whereupon Ouroboros is quelled, Immortalita is freed, and the walls of the cave collapse. Apocalypse! We are suddenly in the Elysian Fields. No wall now separates the land of living Memory from the land of the dead. Immortalita will return to the surface of the Earth, as Persephone does each spring. She will visit the realm of the undying shades only for as long as she likes, thinking always of love on Earth, dreaming languid dreams of love on Earth, addicted to love on Earth, the immemorial inspiration of all poesy on Earth.

Of course I believe in Immortalita. We all do. It is merely a question of when and where and whether we shall meet her.

Novalis, that great poet, also believed in immortality, even though he too was uncertain about the when and where and whether. When his fiancée died at age fifteen he erected an altar to her and he prayed to her, begged that he might die and so be with her. And he did die young, although not until four years later, and by then he was in love with someone else. But he left so much exalted work behind! I thrive on it! I wrote more than one poem to him.

Novalis, your gaze, the holy glance of lonely seer,
Makes itself at home in all the world's places.
The mysteries were there for you alone to hear,
With you ecstatic in prophetic spaces.

Sometimes I dreamed of having night-long conversations with him. We would have become intimate friends, of that I am certain. I would have been his protecting spirit, his guardian angel, as he wanted his fiancée to be.

—If these holes in my lungs allow, Novalis confided to me one night, I will begin work on the second part of *Ofterdingen*. I have a plan now, and I have a theme.

—No more blue flowers for little boys and girls, I teased, but something more for the grownups?

His eyes blazed. He paused, but only for an instant.

—I sense the intelligence of a reader who, looming out of the future, demands more of me than fabulous stuff, something more candid, something more apt and to the point, something for the soul but also for the companionable body.

—If philosophy has its start in the first kiss, as you say, then it is time to reflect on the kisses that follow, kisses that will transform philosophy into a true embrace of science and encyclopedic wisdom.

—I shall return to Saïs, he rejoined, but this time I shall lift a bit higher the skirts of the everliving goddess. May she bear with me. Pen will go to paper in my *Universal Sketchbook* as I go to my lover:

> Sweet whisperings of soft desire
> Are all that we who live require,
> Gazing into eyes that ever bless us,
> Tasting naught than mouth and kisses.

—You give me hope for the future, I said, reciting back to him one of his most trenchant aphorisms.

> A bond that lovers seal unto the death is a marriage—it grants them a comrade for the night. Love is sweetest in death. Death, for the lover, is a wedding night—the secret of sweet mysteries.

> Is it not intelligent to seek for the night a companionable bed?
> If so, then it is also intelligent to reflect that the dearly departed are making love.—

The Dagger

We incised into ourselves a life-and-death pact, a pact of life *unto* death. We formed a union that would endure for all her life, terminating only with her death. She understood that the termination would not be reciprocal. We would not, could not, see one another die. She understood my larger share in immortality. Things endure, people do not. This is what drew her to me in the first place—my patina, my divine aura.

Our pact was not an erotic one, not a pact of love, except in a very attenuated sense. I belonged to her, of course, but not in any slavish way. We would be physical with one another, we always were perfectly physical with each other, but not in any sexual way. We held intercourse with one another, but we had none. You will understand. She was exceedingly proud of me, felt quite close to me, and over the months and years of our pact, I confess, I gradually grew closer to her. I came to respect and even admire her. Tenderness would not be the word. Intense intimacy would be closer to the sense. We were joined like an alloy.

Our pact did not preclude her forming other sorts of pacts, for example, a love pact, even a pact of love *unto* death. Yet this freedom, which I willingly extended to her, did reveal to me the fact that she could make regrettable mistakes, commit absurd errors of judgment.

One glimpse at Creuzer was enough for me. He was no more capable of a love pact, a life-and-death love pact, than an onion. He knew a lot of things from books about the Near East, and that is what impressed us both about him at first. He appreciated that the great Greek civilization would have been nothing without Persia and Egypt and all the peoples of Anatolia and Arabia, from the Golden Crescent all the way to the Indus Valley. Hölderlin too knew that, as did his friend Schelling, and she adored them both for the fact, but how she could have lost her heart to this counterfeit Creuzer, this bad penny, remains a mystery. No, not a penny, nor even an onion. A squash.

This is not jealousy on my part; do not think it. Had she purchased a pistol—that would have evoked jealousy in me. (I feel nothing but contempt for Young Werther, who puts a gun to his head. Such a noise!) If there is a sting of regret I do feel, it lies in the fact that I failed to dissuade her, did not talk some sense into her concerning this gaffe. My damnable, obdurate taciturnity!

And yet, how can I blame myself for all that has happened? She kept her pact with Creuzer a secret, told only one of her friends about it, although that was one too many. She should have learned *perfect* silence from me, and I should have learned *telling* silence from her. I should have imparted to her the burnished wisdom of centuries: do not enter into a love and life and death pact with a bookish squash.

III

Karoline

I studied logic. I filled a notebook with the precepts of this happy science, only to learn that love is sheer contradiction—hapless and hopeless contradiction. There is only one way to dissolve that contradiction, and that is to reaffirm it.

Love

Oh, abundant penury! In giving, blessed retention,
Courage in hesitation! In freedom, detention.
Mute when talking,
By day ever balking,
Victorious in sheer suspension.
Living death, in One alone a life so tender,
In need exultant, in resistance surrender,
Enjoying withering,
Unsated dithering
Life in dreams is redoubled life.

But of all the lives that I have led in books and in dreams, the life of Ariadne on Naxos comes nearest my own. Theseus loves her—after all, she has rescued him from the Old Cow—but he then abandons Ariadne on Naxos and returns to Athens. Ariadne weeps on the Naxian shore. She waits and waits. By rights she should have thrown gravel and stones at him. The god Dionysos arrives now on the island to ravish her. Then he too abandons her. Two of Kronos's three sons approach her. Lightningbolt and Seastorm would make a goddess of her—that is what they promise—but the only Kronide who lures her now is the third son, Hades. Shall Ariadne, Minos's daughter, rise to immortality? Or will she, as a shade, go down to darkling Orkus? Logic here is useless.

Ariadne does not hesitate, she plunges into the sea;
Pain of love betrayed shall not undying be!
Grief does not compel her upward unto godlike might;
A wound to the heart now veils her in graveyard night.

Bettine

Karoline and I often talked about which of the two of us would die first. We would enjoy the ripples of terror that bubbled up our spines when we began such talk. Soon we would feel the terror becoming real. We tried very hard to say *We will see one another die, we will accompany one another in dying*, but we knew it was an impossible sentence, maybe the most impossible sentence, not even Romeo and Juliet could say it. Or, they might murmur it and believe it, but they could never achieve it; they would never be able to synchronize their deaths so that each would witness the other's dying. That is what the tragedy is all about. Liebestod is redoubled frustration.

She wrote me once that she dreamed I had died and that my ghost appeared to her. She spent the next day under tears. The ghosts of her dead sisters too appeared to her, many times, in dreams. She would wake up weeping. She spent much time with the souls of the dead, the *Manes*, as she called them; they were her constant companions, so that when she was alone she was never alone. Only in the presence of the living was she alone.

—Shades! she would say. That is the fruit of all we bear in this life—shades in the land of the dead!

—That is not all there is! I would cry. There is also memory. I would remember you, and you would remember me, wouldn't you?

—Until I myself became a shade, yes. But then we would be together again in the underworld, and we would not need to remember.

—Would we be happy? Happier than Achilles was in death?

That gave her pause. It was a difficult question. And so I asked an easier one.

—You do believe in the spirit world, then?

—I have to. Death is a chemical process, a separation of forces, but not an annihilation of them.

—You and your Schelling! You and your silly Bruno! I cried. But how will we find one another? I mean, after the separation, out there in the dark, how will we find one another?

—We have to start building a community of spirits right now, and we have to keep on building and building.

—But how?

—By developing all our aptitudes together. That's why you have to study your history lessons! You have to read the philosophers! You have to advance to the forefront! Outstanding aptitudes will always find one another on the other side.

—Do you really think so?

—I have to.

Karoline

Apart from my ancient companions and brothers-in-arms, I had two teachers when it came to death and dying. Bruno and Bonaventura they were called. Some people supposed that they were actually the same person, but each of the two assured me that he had nothing to do with the other one and that I should do the same.

Bruno was my guide to the spirit world. Bonaventura, not to be confused with the Seraphic Doctor of the Roman Church, was my cynic. His was the dog's view, and the dog was Cerberus, guardian of the underworld. Bruno's was the god's view. And so I had to read them as a farmer plows his fields, *boustrophedon*, back and forth, forth and back: god dog, dog god, the one after the other, each inverting and contradicting the other. Here too logic was useless.

It is important to believe, to be capable of belief. It is also important not to be duped. It is vital that one be enlightened, and it is crucial to know that all important things are dark: when you shine a light on them you destroy what they are. Love, for example. For another, if it is another, death and dying.

Bruno, or Schelling, was my "adept," or I became his. I copied the entire substance of his *First Projection of a Philosophy of Nature* into my notebook. Perhaps not the *entire* substance of it. Let me be honest. I had no trouble following my dear Bruno to the outermost rim of the crystalline stars. It was the way back down that caused me pain and doubt. I could understand, or at least I believed I understood, that the Absolute could not be an infinite force acting alone, for such a force would dissipate as sheer velocity without being able to produce any effects. It would be a comet's tail, and *physis* would fizzle, as Bettine once quipped. There would have to be a coequally infinite *inhibiting* force that imposed limits on the generative or creative force to produce well-defined, particular things, delineated individuals, and these forces, creation and inhibition, would have to contend with each other for all time to produce the things around us. I had no trouble thinking of these contending forces as love and strife, or attraction and repulsion, the principles behind magnetism and electricity. I had no trouble understanding light and mass as the bearers of these two principles.

I could even understand why the planets not only wander about our sun but also turn on their own axes, whereas our moon, which accompanies us so intimately on our yearly journey, does not spin, so that it keeps the secrets of its dark side.

I could understand that infinite activity cannot be the clenched fist of *being*, that is, sheer contraction, but only the open and extended hand of *becoming*, that is, expansive love. It was also clear why there had to be so little repose in any bounded product of the infinite activity and why that activity had to remain in struggle with inhibition, lest the individual succumb utterly to inertia. The story of my life: either hyperirritability or stupor. If activity were to gain absolute supremacy, the excess of attraction would tighten the fist to paralysis. If inhibition were to gain the upper hand, the excess of repulsion would have—remarkably—the identical deleterious effect, a fist raised against all otherness. How to unclench the fist and open the hand in productive, loving equilibrium, then, is the secret that is sequestered on the dark side of the moon.

I could understand why each element of being had to belong to the totality of the world and why each element must struggle to perfect itself in alignment with the whole. The Absolute alone is bounded by no such belonging. But I had to wonder whether it was lonely. That was silly, of course. The unity of the Absolute would be nothing other than the primordial oneness of the ideal and the real, as of freedom and necessity; all the elements or forces would be inseparable from it and indistinguishable in it, if not in us. The only question that remains is how and why the Absolute began to distinguish and separate its forces: it must have been a free act, an unconstrained decision, since there was nothing to constrain it. That is a bad formulation: it sounds as though there *were* a nothing to constrain it, but nothing is not anything. But then what is inhibition? Inhibition in my own life is what holds me back, what says *no*—and *does* no. I am *not* the Absolute. Stop trying! And yet am I not *of* the Absolute? Am I not its image and likeness? Keep trying! But if there is inhibition as a coeval and coequal force, as there surely is in my own life, then even the Absolute is not absolute.

That is where my problems began, on my way back down from the stars to Charlotte's deathbed. The ancients called nature *physis*, because in it the eternal ideas are *born*. But are they born to die? The fundamental force of nature is the spirit of God being born. But born to die? I could understand the waxing potencies of God, but the impotencies gave me trouble. Did Charlotte introduce these doubts to me? Or was it our father in his narrow box? I do not know. But, once introduced, they could not be expunged.

I remember the point at which my reading of Schelling began to go backward. For I stopped taking notes on his *First Projection* (which was really his *last* projection, his *most recent* projection of a philosophy of nature) as soon as he began to talk of sickness and death, and I went back to reading once again his *World Soul,* and even all the way back to his *Ideas.* I regressed to the cosmic soul and to eternal ideas so that I could avoid his account of the moribund organic, the real world of fragile life confronting a hostile nature, which is where Schelling himself had always been compelled to go. Why did I hesitate? What was it about organic irritability, sensibility, and reproduction that so troubled me? It seemed clear enough that the organic body was the most perfect synthesis of form and essence imaginable, the most perfect synthesis of thinking and being, spirit and mass, the imprint that captures them both most closely by excelling beyond each in separation. But what happens when the waxen matrix of the imprint melts? when the marble of the statue cracks? when form and matter diverge? when spirit and body part ways in delirium and decomposition—as occurs in illness, *mortal* illness?

It was this dark insight—reduced to an appendix at the back of his *First Projection,* but it struck me like a flash of lightning—that illness is not antithetical to nature. Indeed, illness is the most natural thing in the world. The causes of life are, by way of some slight degree of deviation in their proportion, the selfsame causes of death. Life contends against the nature that spawns life, wrests whatever chances it has from nature against nature's own will, so to speak; and nature introduces illness to win back to itself the individuals it may never have wanted to bear. The only proven therapy against mortal illness is therefore death. It is not that the cure is worse than the disease. The cure *is* the disease. The way up is the way down. No wonder my reading regressed to the world soul and ideas. I had felt too keenly the pain of the real. I had carried the slop pail too many times.

Two years before Charlotte died I dreamed that both she and Amalie had succumbed. Years before their demise, their spirits came to me, stepping out of a dark chamber on a rainy November night. Amalie held back, said nothing, but Lotte came directly to me and whispered in my ear.

—An eternally chilly Necessity rules the world, she muttered, not some friendly, loving being.

That dream and its instruction came to me repeatedly over those next two years, until reality caught up with the dream, first Lotte, then Amalie.

76

Their cheekbones and jaws protruding more each day during the last weeks, they seemed to be grinning as they gasped for air. I had to turn away. It was as though light and warmth were penetrating their bodies as pallor and fever, upending their absolute cohesion. It was as though oxygen had become caustic, corrosive negation. They became opaque and went cold. There was no more activity, no life, only a tightfisted being, no becoming, no movement, no dynamism, no struggle except to breathe; nothing was growing in them but death and annihilation, irritability without regeneration, until death came to their rescue and sensibility gave up the ghost altogether. Lotte's spirit appeared to me in a dream once again after her death. *Do not be sad*, she consoled. I could feel the love. But even Bruno says that love—the best of life—is itself but the bridge to death.

Did their souls soar up to the stars or sink into the ground? Did the Earth or mere earth welcome them? Did nature coldly reclaim what it had never wanted to release in the first place—the arrogant life we live, the life that strives so vainly for perfection? And what became of their elements? Were they perfected underground, as I so badly wanted to believe? Or did they disperse in the fetid air? These were the questions that haunted the adept I was convinced I was.

The Adept

Now he can eavesdrop on nature,
Examining her deepest forms;
He knows how materials marry
And how they fuse the ores.

Yet in the end the "adept" is discouraged. Novel details about those deepest workings do not save him. And the final lesson of his philosophy is—what? what can it be?

Novelty has lost its charm.
He knows the Earthmaker's mind,
Yet finds himself alone on Earth.
Humankind is not *his* kind.
Empty now is life's sweet cup,
Yet he lives on, enduring;
The sea he cannot quite give up,
Although his ship is mooring.

He cries, "Woe is he who on the peak
Of life can only motionless stay.
He cannot bear eternal verity—
Happy he who passes all away."

Which left considerable space for Bruno to elaborate and Bonaventura to vituperate.

Bruno

Kant mocked the clairvoyants, ridiculed the spirit seers, and so put us all on our guard. His ascetic philosophy taught him and us to trim all enthusiasms and cut, cut, cut all cant, no pun intended. Delete everything you cannot see hear, touch, taste, or smell! Not that he was a sensualist. He too sensed the action of an inner organ in our heart of hearts, an action that opens us to the presence of benevolent spirits. They are not dead whom our love—though not our fright—can conjure to return.

Who, then, are the dead? What, then, is death? When we die we restore to the earth a more elevated and more highly developed elemental life; the earth continues to shape this life in ever more ascendant forms. And the organism, because it absorbs these continuously developing elements, perforce becomes ever more complete, more perfect, more universal.

True, everything on earth shatters against death—everything, that is, except love. Love is our passport to the spirit world. I lost an adopted daughter. Later I lost her mother. Now their spirits return to me. We converse. We entertain one another. We are intimate. The visiting spirits smile on me and I too smile, with only mild regret over our several solitudes. In those ecstasies, all terror is banished and loneliness becomes a distant memory. Even if the path we mortals have to follow is fraught, our convergence in love—howsoever brief that convergence—is our reward and our sustenance, whether we are philosopher or warrior or poet.

•

For your edification, Bonaventura, and for the edification of us all, I offer some scattered fragments from my aphorisms toward an introduction to the philosophy of nature, which philosophy runs in perfect parallel to a philosophy of spirit:

1. There is no higher revelation, neither in science nor in religion and art, than that of the divinity of the universe; indeed, these other revelations have their commencement and their sole significance in the divinity of the universe.

2. Only when that revelation in fact took place, but then always when it did so, no matter how fleetingly, was there inspiration, a sloughing off of finite forms, the cessation of all dispute, the instauration of unity and of marvelous agreement; such inspiration was intermittent, with long ages intervening, but whenever it arrived it engaged the most unique sorts of individual spirits, the fruit of a general confederation of the arts and sciences. . . .

23. Poesy too is philosophy, but not of the precocious sort that resounds in a mere subject; rather, an intrinsic poesy is cultivated in the *object*, as in the case of the music of the spheres. The matter itself first of all is poetic, long before it comes to word. . . .

89. Mass creates the body . . . but not the shadow that the body casts on another body or that other bodies cast on it. . . . Shadow derives from light. . . .

96. The divine universe is not merely the spoken word, but the speaking word itself, not the created but the very creating, revealing itself in an infinite way. . . .

125. Through birth, a lifetime lived, and a death, each of these in accord with the divine order, every creature pays its debt to sheer finitude, its being contained in God. The creature exists in time only with as much of its self as is *relation* in it, and only what has been annihilated in God will be annihilated in the creature through time. . . .

159. The intellect, suffering vertigo as it stands on the abyss of the question *Why is there not nothing? why is there anything at all?* discovers that the fully valid answer lies not in the *anything* but in the universe, or God. . . .

163. This is the secret of eternal love: In the case of whatever would want to be absolute for itself, it would nonetheless never be considered a deprivation if it were to be for itself in such a way that it is absolute only in and with others. If each were not a whole but only a part of the whole, there would not be love: but there is love precisely because each is a whole and nevertheless is not and cannot be without the other. . . .

224. The smallest thing, like the greatest, is holy both by way of its inner infinity and by way of the fact that in accord with its eternal ground and its being in the universe it cannot be annihilated, lest the infinite whole itself as such be annihilated.

•

Master these thoughts, Bonaventura, and you will achieve all that is best for humans. You will be happier in your living and in your dying.

Bonaventura

I soon gave up on poetry—it was like trying to breathe in a room full of feathers—and philosophy turned out to be the exploded pillow that had released all those suffocating feathers—and so I became a night watchman. Now I call out the hours after nightfall and I peek through the windows at the sick and the dying in their houses. In every case a quack physician hovers at the bedside trying to peddle his final philtres and powders before it is too late, and there on the other side of the bed is the local pastor, already dressed in black, fit to kill, ready to mourn but desperate to squeeze out a final tithe from the moribund. The pastor gives the dying man the Good News. Let us listen in. For that is what will edify us.

—The spirit world awaits you. But you cannot enter, Sinner! with your pockets laden with gold. Divest! Divest to the Lord, that your soul may soar and not be dragged down by the weight of filthy lucre!

Throughout the hours of the night and from door to door, window to window, I witness the pious extortion, and I watch the stricken succumb. Oh, but the pastor is not finished. More Good News.

—Love conquers death. Only believe and you will be saved. But do give us a sign of your deliverance, a material sign of love.

Wheedling and cajoling, mollifying and terrifying the moribund by turns through the night—and it is a moonless night—the drama repeats itself endlessly. Before I can ring in the dawn, which is still so uncertain, the neophyte widow bends over the corpse, tears of love flowing freely from her swollen eyes.

And is death then conquered? *O death where is thy prick?* mumbles the pastor. He does not press the question lest death make reply. We see the widow hesitate. Perhaps her husband is a difficult case? She opens her narrow purse. Perhaps a few pennies more in the pastor's coffers will turn the trick?

•

As for your edifying aphorisms, my dear Bruno, I reply, respectfully and in all modesty:

81

23 + 96 + 125 = 0. God has made a garrulous lifetime out of this speaking and materializing as the Word, cultivating himself in matter and in speech, until the botched Creation lies before him and us, the product of a wretched speech defect. And in the throes of love the Word became flesh, they say. It had come to that pass. What was the matter with him, the material in him? What did God have to annihilate in himself? And why did he need us to do it for him over time?

89 + 125 + 224 = 0. What shadow was cast on God? On whom could his white light cast a shadow, and who could cast a shadow on him? What exactly did he have to "annihilate" in himself? My own lifetime, perhaps? But will that save him? Or all our lifetimes? If he were to live at all in this heart of mine, or that heart of yours, would that shelter him? Is he that needy? So it seems. One day, dear Bruno, you will confront the nightmare of God's pathetic loneliness—the fact that there is Nothing out there for him—and you will awaken amid the rubble of your detonated system.

163 x 2 = 0. Let us dwell a moment longer on the mystery of eternal love. There *is* love, not because each lover is a whole but because each lover is a hole, that is, because each lover is lacerated and needs the other to lick its wounds. What is this infernal neediness in all of us? What is this unquenchable thirst, this insatiable hunger, this terrible longing? What is *desire*? What is its devilishly divine source, do you suppose? Only this much is certain: we languish, we lie stretched on the rack and wheel of yearning; if we refuse to confess this, it is only because cowardice cripples us. The mystery of eternal love is not that it never lasts but that it never commenced. What endures is the neediness, the wound, the hole. Listen to what a cooler head says:

—Love is the most monstrous contradiction, one that the intellect cannot solve, insofar as there is nothing more solid to depend on than this unique point of self-consciousness which in each case is my own; that point gets negated when we love, even though I ought to be able to possess that point and affirm it forever. Love is at once the instantiation and the dissolution of the contradiction.

In a word, and more precisely thought than even the coolest head can think it, love is the ontological boondoggle—the tragic end of absolutely any Absolute one might have hoped to make credible. There is no point trying to evade the inevitable. You dream of freedom, but you waken in *need*. You dream of love, but aching *desire* made the world. One day you will break down and confess it. And there once again, scattered all around you, will be the debris of your system.

159 = 159 = 159. There is not nothing. There is some thing. But it is not any old thing. That thing is *need*, shadowed by *desire*. The vertigo is not only in you but also in the universe, or God. This is so—at least if the smallest particle in the universe is equal to the whole and if that particle cannot be eliminated from the universe without the tremulous whole collapsing. Imagine, if you can, a *company* of gods and goddesses, companions since birth from a common mother, equal in number and in power. If one of them should find herself shadowless in the world of shades, defunct, how could the others bear it? If one should die, all would go under. How can she avoid the terrifying consequence that an entire world collapses in her own catastrophe? If something in God has to be annihilated—a birth, a lifetime lived, a sex, a death—then it will be she. But do not deceive yourself with vulgar misogyny: all will come tumbling after.

•

You yourself, dear Bruno, will have written the truth about human nature, human history, and humankind. I need only urge you to develop your thinking a few paces more. Then you will have to say:

—The lot of the world and of humankind is BY NATURE a tragic lot, and every tragic event that transpires in the course of the world is but a variation on its single grand theme, which continuously renews itself. The deed to which all suffering may be attributed did not occur once and for all; it is what is always and eternally HAPPENING.

And as you continue to grow and mature, dear Bruno, you will note that the production of the tragedy mirrors the producer. If your God is the source of all that happens, then he or she will share that tragic lot—indeed your God and every possible God *is* that tragic lot.

Karoline

We are of a piece with nature, as Bruno says. The proof is that whenever we do not know what we are doing nature guides us and it is as though we do know after all. When I, who know nothing about lovemaking, because I was never permitted to know the slightest thing about it, see the wide opening at the throat of his white blouse, I know exactly what to do. My lips and tongue astonish me with their know-how. My wisdom amazes me when he sprawls at my side. In the viewless night my body has the keenest sight and the boldest wit. He fumbles, I dance.

Things are better now, things are clearer now that I know our Benefactress will not grant him a divorce after all. Earlier on, she had answered my candid letters by saying she would relinquish her claim on him—holy love demanded its rights, and she would bow to love. She has now reneged. But all is well. Things are now more sane. We will not form a ménage à trois with her, living together in Heidelberg à la bohème; we will not scandalize his colleagues at the university, which is his gravest fear. Creuzer and I will not be fleeing to Russia as we had planned, with me disguised as a boy. We will not have children.

The truth is that I never wanted to marry him. It was he who pushed the idea. Yet it is not as though I do not love him: whenever my trusted friends (only a woman can understand another woman) let us use their rooms or find us some other hidden spot—today in a back room of St. John's Inn in Reichelsheim—he comes to me as he will come to me in just a few moments, bleating for my breasts and my sex, sucking at me everywhere for whatever he thinks he can find and, even as he fumbles, invariably finding it. I faint with pleasure. No, not pleasure. Too weak a word for too strong a feeling. Electric shock. Lightningbolt ecstasy. Quake. Cataclysm. Convulsion. No. Not even that. No words. Deeds. Utter submission to deeds. Deeds undertaken against the tide and in the face of the storm.

We are of a piece with nature.

Nothing can separate us.

Not even death.

The White Slippers

We have seen him kissing her feet and we are of four minds about it. On the right side, he is to be lauded for having made a series of correct decisions. Our Karoline is exquisite, and no part of a woman is as exquisite as the foot. We say that not to disparage the other excellences, all of which are admirably conceived and marvelously wrought, but to conform to what persons of a philosophical cast of mind have affirmed throughout the ages. For precisely that reason, however, we can, on the left side, the sinister side, scarcely abide his encroachments and incursions. We do not find him worthy. We confess to a tinge of jealousy, but our judgment is not thereby muddied or confused. He is unworthy.

He worships the ground she walks on, that is true, so let him kiss the ground. Her feet, we find, are too perfect for his pinched and pallid pucker! There is something too hurried about his osculatory gesture, as though he wants those kisses to wander off elsewhere. And wander off they do. We have to avert our gaze. We close our eyelets. When a man is in Paradise he should not yearn to head for other parts. We find him profligate. We find him promiscuous.

The splendid cathedrals, the towering mosques and synagogues of the civilized world imitate her vaulted arch. Her heel is far too delicate to crush serpents. Her instep is a porch of Pantelic marble on a palace of Pallas. Her toes are what fingers yearn to be but never quite achieve; they are peninsulae of the Promised Land. We listen in on and are amused by the foolish debates as to whether, for beauty's sake, the second toe, the index, dare exceed the big toe in length. Observe the feet that step out of Botticelli's studio and, having observed, collapse in awe and wonderment! It is not a matter of relative length; it is a matter of ubiquitous delicacy. Whether it is Flora or Venus or Galatea on a half-shell or Maria being crowned the Queen of Heaven by both the Father and the Son, the index points to deity, and we conform to the deity of beauty alone, as you too must conform to it.

You ask us how it is with *her* feet, the specific feet of our chosen mistress, but we betray no secrets, at least not by any word of ours. We do not need to speak. We conform to her delightful form utterly. All you

85

need do is study our assumed shapes and all your burning questions will be answered, your ardent curiosity satisfied. Your fetish is our everydayness. Take a deep breath, a long and pensive inhalation. Do you wonder at the scent of hyacinth? Do not be astonished. We are not slipshod. We too are of God.

Karoline

Last night I had a bizarre dream, a dream I cannot forget. I was lying in my bed, a lion lay to my right, a she-wolf to my left, and a bear at my feet; all three were half-draped over me, all but I were deep in slumber, but I could not budge. I was thinking that if these animals were to awaken each would be enraged by the presence of the others; they would tear one another apart and me with them. I was terrified, but I managed ever so slowly to wriggle my way out from underneath them, whereupon I dashed off to safety. The dream seems to be an allegory. What is one to make of it?

•

The Lion Speaks: I lie at her right side, the masculine side, the side of pure will and willpower. I am an agent of philosophy. I am the avatar of heroic literature. I am her writing hand. The pads of my right paw rest on her right arm, but during the day I guide her writing. I am her amanuensis. She counts on me, the king of beasts, to be steadfast, stalwart, and unshakable, while she in her own heart of hearts vacillates, retreats, is shaken down to her shoes and blown away by every breeze. My claws are withdrawn in the night, never fear, she is safe, but she counts on those same claws to tear and eviscerate when daylight brings on the hunter. My name is *Leo*. In a better world I would be lying with the lamb. But in this world I share the lamb and the space of her sheepish dreams with rougher bedmates.

The She-Wolf Speaks: I sleep to her left, the side sinister. And sinister I am, utterly uncanny, a rogue and renegade lycophantasm, a slouching lone wolf. I roam with no pack. To the others, all others, I show my curling lip, my flashing teeth, my hypnotic eye. I crouch. I am sly and sudden. No one drives me, for I *am* drive, I alone urge and urge. I am push and pull, tug and thrust. I am the force behind all you are doing when you know not what you do. My name is *Lupa*. Myself without wolf cubs, I nursed the Roman twins with the milk of war and empire, I nurtured their drive to conquer. And when the conquests faltered, when the heroes fumbled, I braced the sword on which they fell. My slender paw sometimes slips across her belly. Right now it is draped over her rib cage. Between four and five.

The Bear Speaks: I hibernate. My body temperature sinks to the bare minimum, my metabolism slows to the ticking of a weary wintertime clock. Yet if my temperature should plunge too low, I stir. My profound hunger makes me irritable, and my irritability makes me very dangerous. If I should rise and stand on my hind feet and roar my earth-shaking roar, my bedmates three would tremble in terror and then scatter. But I hibernate. I keep her feet warm, her toes nestle in my neck fur. My paw is draped over a shapely knee. My name is either *Ursula* or *Oberon*, depending on whether I am a sow or a boar. If you are curious to know which of the two I am—presuming, as I do not, that these two nominations, borrowed haphazardly from other beasts, are apt and that there are always only two definable sexes, *either* female *or* male—you might of course approach me and investigate. I do understand your need to decide, your need to determine, your nervousness. But I urge caution.

•

My guardian spirit has deserted me, I drift and concoct the strangest plans. I am restless, and everything seems foreign to me. Creuzer himself seems foreign to me now, not so much with regard to my feelings for him, but because of the gap that I know separates us. I see things more clearly now. I see that I am a fugitive, cast out of my native land, and that I am as little at home in my own thoughts as I was that night among the beasts in my dream.

I notice more than ever that my heroic soul has dissolved in the tepid brew of love's tenderness and love's longing. Such a condition is not good for a human being who, now that she will never be joined to the object of her love, has to stand on her own two feet. Resignation is no long-term solution, even if I deceive myself repeatedly about this. It is bizarre, but I often possess the beloved object in my thoughts so totally that I am convinced, down to every last detail, that one day my thoughts will become reality. When such paroxysms pass, I repair to the slough of despond.

Goethe

After Bettine, in that irritatingly chaotic way of hers, told me about her deceased young friend, I went back to my library and dug out her little book of poems and fantasies, the book I had found so strange, so remarkable, when I first read it through. The pages fell open to "An Apocalyptic Fragment," where I had jotted some remarks in the margins about Schelling's philosophy and the First Book of Moses, which some call "Genesis." It all came back to me as I read her pages once again.

The strangest thing of all is the deliberate numbering of the passages: fifteen carefully articulated steps into a totally disarticulated world, a seemingly well-ordered entry into a chimerical universe of unchanging change, where time itself becomes untimely and the very paste of things dissolves. It is as though the Demiurge were murmuring to himself; he is on the very eve of Creation but then changes his mind. He turns aside and broods.

1. I was standing on a high peak on the Mediterranean shore, before me the east, behind me the west, and the wind at rest on the sea.

2. The sun sank behind me, but scarcely had it veiled itself in downgoing when the morn dawned again, and morning, noon, evening, and night chased one another across the arc of the sky at a dizzying pace.

3. Astonished, I watched the phases of the cycle in wild spin, and yet my pulse did not fly any faster, my thoughts did not move any more quickly, and the time within me flowed at its usual pace, while outside of me it seemed to be moving according to a new law.

4. I wanted to plunge into the red dawn of day or dive into the shadows of the night, to be drawn into their hurry, and not to live so sluggishly; but as I continued to observe them I grew weary and drifted off to sleep.

5. I then saw the wide sea opening before me with no surrounding shore either to the east or south or west or north:

no puff of wind ruffled the surface, but the immeasurable sea stirred in its depths, as though troubled by some inner ferment.

6. And a number of shapes emerged from the womb of the deep sea as swaths of fog rose and became clouds; the clouds then descended and stung with lightning flashes the waves that were giving birth to them.

7. And still more figures, manifold shapes, emerged from the depths; vertigo seized me, and a peculiar terror; my thoughts were driven hither and thither like a torch flame in a windstorm, until my memory was extinguished.

8. When I came to and began to apprehend something about where I was, I still did not know how long I had been asleep, whether it was for centuries or mere minutes; even though I had been having dark and turbulent dreams, I encountered nothing now that could have reminded me of the time.

9. But I had an obscure feeling that I had been reposing in the womb of this sea and had now emerged from it, as all the other shapes had. To myself I seemed a drop of dew, and I danced here and there in the air, and I felt happy that the sun was mirroring itself in me and the stars were gazing down on me.

10. I let the breezes carry me off in their sudden drafts, I kept company with the sunset, and I lined up with my droplet friends, the seven colors of the rainbow, and we spun around the moon even as it tried to hide. We accompanied the lunar orb in its orbit.

11. The past had vanished from me! I belonged to the present alone. But a yearning was in me—for what I did not know. I was longing ceaselessly, but everything I found was not what I was looking for, and, ever yearning, I plunged headlong into the infinite.

12. At some point I realized that all the creatures that earlier on had emerged from the ocean had by now returned to it

and that they were reproducing themselves in ever-mutating forms. This phenomenon alarmed me, for I could not envisage how it all would end. Then it struck me that my yearning too was the longing to return to the source of life.

13. And when I thought this, feeling almost more alive than my own consciousness could know, a numbing fog suddenly buried my heart of hearts. But the fog soon vanished, and I seemed to be no longer myself and yet more myself than ever before. I could no longer locate my boundaries; my consciousness had advanced beyond all bounds; it had become otherwise; it had become something far more magnificent; and yet I could still feel my self in it.

14. I had been released from the narrow confines of my essence, and I was no longer a mere droplet. I had been delivered over to all things once again, and every thing belonged to me as well. I thought and felt that I was cradled in the ocean, glistening in the sun, turning with the stars. I felt my self in all things and I enjoyed all things in me.

15. And so, who has ears to hear, let him hear! It is not a matter of two, or three, or a thousand; it is one and all. It is not body and soul in separation, such that the one belongs to time, the other to eternity. It is all one, belonging to itself, and it is time and eternity at once; it is visible and invisible, enduring in transition, an infinite life.

Had I known this uncanny young woman before her undoing, I would have worried myself to death about her. If Bettine's description of her person is apt, and if her portrait of this Orphic poetess is even close to the truth, I would have felt much more than worry.

Bettine

I hated her apocalypse, hated it, hated it, hated it! Her place is down here with me, not sailing off to the infinite—that way lies death. I do not know much, but I know that. She had sent those pages to me with a letter. I loved the letter, but I scorned her apocalypse, and I was not shy about telling her so in my next letter.

—You always show up right on time to put me on the straight path and show me how stupid I have been. I suppose I should be grateful. But your "philosophical essay," as you call it, I am sending right back to you. You can have it; I cannot use it. You know what I call it? I call it a dried-up snippet scribbled by a hedge-high dwarf, a nasty troll, a sickening green worm lodged in the throat, a pestilence of puffed-up empty talk, devoid of music, all cacophony and mocking laughter—don't make me crazy, don't send me this kind of stuff. You knew I would hate it so why did you send it?

Seriously. Why do you send me things you know I will never understand? Are you trying to make me feel obtuse? (I know, you'll tell me that making me feel obtuse is too easy! You are right about that, you are always right, no need to rub my nose in it.) Your proper place, if you want to know, is in the doorway watching me clamber up trees and scaring you half to death with my daredevil tricks. You pay me back by frightening me with these ridiculous ideas and jagged dreams. Your words make me dizzy. They sting my eyes, they box my ears, they are bitter in my mouth.

Be sweet to me! You seek your playmates now among rainbow dewdrops? Why am I suddenly not enough for you? You say you feel too confined, that you want to shatter the boundaries of your self? We all have boundaries, accept them! The only thing in the world that has no boundaries is my love for you, accept it! Stay here with me! My entire happiness lies in those boundaries that make you the particular you that you are. You don't have to chase the moon in her orbit. That's lunacy! And you certainly don't have to chase me. Walk with me up the hill to our familiar friendly fortress and we'll let the moon enrapture us both. We'll hold hands. I will kiss your mouth. What more could the moon do for you?

I admit it. I am hopelessly jealous. Of what I do not know. But how can I not be jealous? I know how flighty you find me, you've always told me that plainly enough. I know I have not got the mind you want me to have. But do you have to be so condescending, so insulting to someone who loves you better than any inflated thoughts can ever love you? Come back down, walk on the Earth that I walk on, even if I am a fool, a jealous fool. Be kind to fools! That's why we are here!

Your apocalypse makes me afraid that you will turn me away some day, that we are together only for an instant of this life, that you will someday repulse me. And then what am I to do? You used to dream about me, you told me so, and now you mock me because I live in a smaller world, a not so dreamily vast world; I can see only what is right in front of me, but it is you I see. Always and always! Time and eternity are both too big. You say you want to swim in the ocean. Swim in me! No unholy phantoms are creeping out of me! You want the ever-changing? I want the never-changing. You make me feel all tumbled and jumbled. Don't do this to me!

You yearn for higher regions, for the upper air, you want friends who can dance around the lunar orb, where I can never go? You should be dancing with me! With me, down here, dancing as we always do, you being Günter and me the loving beloved. You long to be released from your limitations, your peculiarities? What if I love those peculiarities?! I am repeating myself, but that is your fault.

You say I am immature. I'm young, that's all, give me time, give me love, stay! Stay on the ground where I am. Chase after the moon like this and I promise I will scorch you with the jealousy that burns in me. Or I will bite your hand again—you remember?—and make you cry.

If you find me childish, infantile even, well then, you who are so smart, you who understand everything, you do not understand the infant who sucks at your breast. I at least understand that this is how it is going to be for the rest of my life. Don't toss me out of my cradle!

Fare thee well!

The Dagger

I detest histrionics. An ably constructed drama—a *Maria Stuart* or a *Tasso*, even a well-told *Ali Baba*—is one thing, but histrionics are another. When men fight, someone dies, usually at my hand. When women fight, it is all histrionics. All for show, bad theater, circus. It is as though they cannot wait for the hairpulling to end so they can collapse into one another's arms and make love.

Now, it was not that bad between Karoline and Bettine, but it came close, as I witnessed. I did not get to see the end of it—I wound up under the sofa licking my own wounds—but I could hear them on top of me. However, let me start at the beginning.

Karoline had purchased me at the Easter Fair in Frankfurt some months after Charlotte's death late in 1801, a death that had much affected Karoline. Not only affected her but infected her as well. It seemed likely that her sister's tuberculosis attacked Karoline's eyes: they were chronically reddened after that, and her vision deteriorated. I am certain that she was drawn to me for a profound reason. She kept me in her clothes closet for the most part, but on bad nights, when her courage was low, we slept together. I was happy to be able to ease her troubled heart. I was less happy when she would fetch me out of the closet to show me to some visitor she was trying to impress. Histrionics. I hated it. She exhibited me to Achim and to Bettine more than once. Achim would wrestle with her, Bettine would make a fuss, more histrionics, and then I would go back into the closet. No harm done.

Not on that evening, however. On that evening in early May 1803, not long after another sister's death—Amalie, I believe—Karoline took me out of the closet. She was complaining to Bettine about how lonely her life had become, what with everyone dying on her and her sly mother absconding with her paternal inheritance. But then she surprised Bettine—and me as well.

—I've been to see a surgeon, said Karoline. He gave me very precise instructions.

She was wearing a smile that did not become her and that did not please me. Nor did it please Bettine.

—Stop it! cried Bettine. You know I hate it when you do this!

But Karoline did not stop. She unbuttoned her dress and slipped the white chemise off her shoulder. With her left hand she cupped and lifted her left breast. The nipple was very alert.

—This line of shadow, she said, marks the spot.

She pointed me there. I could feel her warmth.

Bettine cried out, and as quickly invented a stratagem.

—Let me see it! demanded Bettine.

I did not mind the neuter pronoun. That is the way humans talk. Karoline handed me to her carefully by the hilt. Bettine ran her index finger along the edge of me to see how sharp I was. She was clearly a girl who had never held a creature like me in her hands before. Instead of running her thumb crosswise over my edge, feeling the graininess and the subtle vibrations that would tell her everything she needed to know about me, she ran her finger lengthwise along me and immediately drew blood. It may have been intentional, I do not know. It is not my affair to know. If you ask me in, I enter.

—You silly girl, look what you've done! cried Karoline.

Bettine was the one to smile now, as though she had won some sort of victory.

—You're always playing the heroine, cried Bettine, and now you run at the sight of blood!

And so it was. Karoline dashed into the bedroom to find a swath of gauze.

—It is all play-acting with you, Bettine railed. What have you got to do with keen steel? It's nothing but a stage prop. But look at it! It's real! It's as pointy as a needle and as sharp as a razor! It's nothing for an actress. Why do you keep it here? Why all this theater?!

Bettine rattled on while Karoline, having returned, wrapped Bettine's finger attentively, which in any case was bleeding less. I had been modest.

—It is my talisman, Karoline said quietly. It helps me. It counsels me during the worst times.

—What nonsense! growled Bettine. Talisman? Counsel? It makes no sense.

—Does everything have to make sense? And does something have to be harmful just because it looks dangerous?

By this time Bettine was in tears, but not because of the wound to her finger. She was good at getting herself all riled up. And Karoline was certainly not helping.

—You're supposed to be my teacher! cried Bettine under tears. You're to tell me what life is all about. And then you show me this thing, you hurt me with it. You know I would die for you, and still you do this to me. If you came to my window at midnight and tossed a pebble and called to me to come down, I would run off with you, you know I would, to anywhere in all the world!

Bettine was still holding me in her right hand, gesticulating all the while, incautiously if the truth be told. Suddenly she lifted me high, wielding me at eye level. It reminded me of that magnificent scene in *Macbeth*.

> Is this a dagger which I see before me,
> The handle toward my hand? Come, let me clutch thee.
> I have thee not, and yet I see thee still.
> Art thou not, fatal vision, sensible
> To feeling as to sight? or art thou but
> A dagger of the mind, a false creation,
> Proceeding from the heat-oppressed brain?
> I see thee yet, in form as palpable
> As this which now I draw.

Of course, Macbeth and his Lady knew what a dagger is for. These two children, Karoline and Bettine, were entirely innocent.

—Give it back, commanded Karoline, ever so quietly.

She covered her breast now and extended her right hand. But that double gesture set off a spark in Bettine, who exploded into a rage. She backed away from Karoline, wielding me now in front of her, almost threateningly.

—I won't! I'd rather use this on you than see you use it on yourself. I won't let you abandon me!

With that, she moved menacingly toward Karoline. It seemed to me absurdly melodramatic, comical really, completely ridiculous, but Karoline did not laugh. She backed away.

—Give it back!

—I won't! I'll use it! On you and then on myself!

Karoline spun about and hurried into her bedroom. But before she could shut the door Bettine was right there, holding me high. Karoline took cover behind her reading chair. I began to be mildly concerned. You never know what amateurs will do when they get carried away.

Bettine dashed over to the chair, an ancient lumpy upholstered thing where Karoline used to read and study, often with Bettine on her lap. Bettine plunged me into the chair over and over again, horsehair and dust flying everywhere, Bettine grunting with the effort, Karoline crying out.

—My poor chair!

—I'll not stop till the knife is dull!

I hate it when people call me a knife, as though I were a menial. But I was too full of stuffing to pay much attention to the insult.

Karoline moved deftly around the chair and grasped Bettine's arm. They tussled. Bettine was a little thing, Karoline much taller. But Bettine was feisty, and Karoline was faery-like, what we call a *Péri*. I could not foresee how this might end.

Karoline gave Bettine's arm a vigorous shake and I found myself flying through the air, out the bedroom door, and onto the wooden floor of the parlor. I scudded along, winding up under the sofa, a bit rattled and bruised but otherwise undamaged.

I saw Bettine's feet dashing toward me, with Karoline's slippered feet right behind hers. More tussling, more sobs. Then the two of them collapsed on the sofa above me. Still more sobs. Some undecipherable sounds. Then quiet.

Night came on.

Goethe

I often have the sense that I am being visited by the dead—that the dead come to speak again in my characters. Such visitations become more frequent and more commanding as a persona becomes more prominent in the drama, when her or his role in the storyline grows more significant. It is then that the dead take over my process. Nowhere was this more true than in the case of Ottilie.

So many visitations from the dead occurred as she came to life in me. The cranky old crone who complains about Ottilie's reticence, about the girl's too eager willingness to serve, about the young woman's wish to remain inconspicuous, to disappear in a crowd of others who are struggling to stand out from the crowd, about her moderation in eating and drinking, as though these things were faults—that old crone rose from her grave to tell me all that. Another neighbor from Frankfurt, long dead, returned to tell me of Ottilie's frequent headaches (on the left side, I believe, just above the eye), which often distracted her, so that she sometimes seemed dull-witted—*Good heavens! cries Ottilie's tutor, How can someone look so stupid when she isn't?!* My great uncle, now dust, told me very early on that Ottilie had been raised in an "adoption home." That was his expression. The dead were so well informed about her! She was beautiful, they said, but as an unripe fruit is beautiful, her capabilities undeveloped, her perfections unpolished, her excellences borderline hindrances, her blessings potentially fatal curses, at least in this caricature of a world in which she will have to survive. And Ottilie took to heart all the absurd grievances of these others. The picture of grace, she seemed to herself clumsy; she never botched things, but she was forever afraid she might. She held back her judgments, but when by chance they escaped from her they were always apt, her finger on the map touched the precise spot.

I think back to that conversation with Bettine about the young woman Bettine had loved, and loved passionately. It seemed to involve a magnetism that Bettine herself never understood, an unaccountable visitation, as though from the already dead—the daemonic, τὸ δαιμόνιον, young Schelling would say. Be that as it may, we never elect the affinities. They elect us.

Affinities? Visitations? I believe the spiritists call them *channelings*. They run along the links of a magnetized chain. What people mistake as inspiration is this magnetism. Young Schelling tells of that too in his nature books. We are not "inspired." Let us not inflate our importance. We are all mere iron filings drawn by and to the magnet. Ottilie herself wanders in a state of perpetual magnetization. The development of her character shows this as the story proceeds; her challenge is to become hospitable to her destiny. Her fate hangs on her accepting her own magnetism. Failing that, hers will be an untimely death.

The Dagger

We daggers do not reproduce sexually. We retain our dignity. We have no family, hence no family stories as such. Yet we do have the legends of our guild, if I may put it that way. One of the oldest legends is that of Lucretia, whose dagger founds the Roman Republic. I shall recount the story here in all brevity.

Kings ruled in Italy long before Rome became a name and acquired a fame, long before both the Empire and the Republic, long before the Caesars. At one point, Tarquin the Superb ruled as king, but he was less superb than his name implied. Another Tarquin, a dastardly scion of the Superb, offended the laws of hospitality by raping his host's wife. Lucretia donned a black toga the following morning and went to her husband Collatine and to her father as a suppliant, begging their forgiveness even though she was faultless. She demanded that they rouse the people to revolt and banish the entire brood of Tarquins and establish the Republic. Of course, they did forgive her. What was there to forgive?

> But al for noght; for thus she seide anoon,
> "Be as be may," quod she, "of forgiving,
> I wol nat have no forgift for no-thing."
> But prively she caughte forth a knyf,
> And therwith-al she rafte her-self her lyf.

Husband and father had given her their word that the Tarquins would be ousted, whereupon, as we have heard the poet only now say, she plunged a dagger—the poet calls it "a knyf" but it is a dagger she has concealed beneath that funereal toga—into her heart. A later poet describes the aftermath of the gory scene, in details that, forgive me, I have to relish.

> Stone-still, astonish'd with this deadly deed,
> Stood Collatine and all his lordly crew;
> Till Lucrece' father, that beholds her bleed,
> Himself on her self-slaughter'd body threw;
> And from the purple fountain Brutus drew

100

The murderous knife, and, as it left the place,
Her blood, in poor revenge, held it in chase;

And bubbling from her breast, it doth divide
In two slow rivers, that the crimson blood
Circles her body in on every side.

Brutus—not Caesar's Brutus, but some early ancestor of that later more famous one—holds high the crimsoned dagger and swears an oath:

By this bloody knife,
We will revenge the death of this true wife.

The poet closes the scene most colorfully.

This said, he struck his hand upon his breast,
And kiss'd the fatal knife, to end his vow;
And to his protestation urged the rest.

I tremble at his kiss! Lucretia's fame as a virtuous and dutiful wife was established; her savvy in matters of polity and governance was also evident. Her death would induce the birth of the Republic. Her double desecration—the first by Tarquin,

With Tarquin's ravishing strides, towards his design
Moves like a ghost,

the second by her own hand—that redoubled desecration of the woman sealed the fate of the Tarquinian kings. Rome never wearied of celebrating Lucretia and her blood-drenched dagger. A thousand painters have painted her and me. Myriad poets sing her praises, exulting in her fidelity, her courage, and her handiwork—in a word, her metal.

The Confessor

Those same poets, however, give us pause. They give us reason to doubt. If her heart did not to some degree accede to the rape, then why does she prick that agitated heart? When she threw herself upon the mercy of both husband and father, and when both expressed most sincerely their forgiveness, why could she not accept that mercy? "I wol nat have no forgift for no-thing," she says. But was it really no-thing? Why then did she throw herself upon her sword, as it were, rather than on the mercy that was so freely proffered by two noble generations? The first poet says that with the "knyf" Lucretia "raffte her-self her lyf." But *raffen* derives from *rapere*, "rape." She therefore does not avenge her rape but redoubles it. The later poet confirms this:

> She bears the load of lust he left behind,
> And he the burden of a guilty mind.

Why can she not disburden herself of that load of lust? Does she not in fact share the burden of a guilty mind? Does not her second deed prove participation in the first? Her cruel death, the ravaging of her body and her soul—was it simply the result of a faulty calculation on her part? The poet tries out this ploy on the unreflective spectator.

> Thy wretched wife mistook the matter so,
> To slay herself, that should have slain her foe.

Mistook? Let us reflect. Tarquin's deed was black as night. Lucretia's deed was black as pitch. The proof lies in the punishment. For he was merely banished for his deed, whereas she committed a homicide against herself. The sin of the first can be forgiven, granted proper repentance; the sin of the second is beyond repentance and every possible restitution.

No doubt the pagan Romans, after displaying her bloodied corpse in the senate, gave her a stately burial. Had she lived in our more enlightened time, an age illumined by the one true Faith, we would have buried her inverted—head downward, so that she might never come to rest—in unconsecrated ground, where fox and jackal might feast on her bones. Ours is the more profound justice, the longer-lasting, the unforgiving.

Had she thrown herself on the mercy of a Heavenly Father, instead of on that mere mortal one, she would surely have acquiesced in His infinite mercy and not committed the sinful violation of herself. To be sure, she lived half-a-millennium too early, and that cannot be held against her. Yet there is little doubt, as our most illustrious Church Father argues, that she was not nearly as guiltless as the many Christian virgins and martyrs who died at the hands of the cruel Romans; there can also be little doubt that she was not as guiltless as she claimed to be; little doubt that "the relic of Eve" that lies concealed in the maculate bodies of all mortal women since our expulsion from Paradise was at work in her as well. What does she herself say of her much-celebrated "honor"?

> "My honour I'll bequeath unto the knife
> That wounds my body so dishonoured.
> 'Tis honour to deprive dishonour'd life."

A sophism of the worst sort. There is no honor in dishonoring life, and hers was the graver dishonor. For her murderous deed was at best an act of wounded pride, not of true contrition, and pride is a grave sin. Nor is this her final sophism, her last sin against humility.

> Mine honour be the knife's that makes my wound;
> My shame be his that did my fame confound.

To claim that honor adheres to an implement of destruction—how utterly absurd! Unfeeling, unthinking, unrelenting, the dagger is a thing without life or wit, a soulless thing outside the realm of Grace, a material item condemned to rust and dissolution!

Yet there is more; there is worse. If shame confounds her fame, as she proclaims, then that shame cannot be attributed entirely to Tarquin. In her heart of hearts she knows this, and that heart becomes the target of her vengeance. She adorns herself in the raiment of night and conceals a deadly weapon against the flesh of her person. That is to say, *she premeditates*. The benighted Romans, the pagans who have caused the Children of God so much suffering, celebrate her so-called perfection.

But no perfection is so absolute,
That some impurity doth not pollute.

Quod erat demonstrandum.

Friedrich Creuzer

Creuzer to Günderrode: O you sacred soul! magnificent essence! my spirit bows before you! Heaven, not Earth, is your fatherland, that is where you came from to console me, but to the world you are as an alien visitor. Do not count on being understood by the world. But I understand you and I have been permitted to love you and I am allowed to say that I love you! O you pristine creature, how fond of you I am!

How gladly would my spirit, oblivious to all the conditions of reality and blessed by its possession of the most excellent one, freely hover over the oppressive atmosphere of Earth. Is it his fault if an envious god has dragged his spirit down? Delivered over to a marriage that by nature could never be a marriage, I was aware of nothing else than an unfulfilled longing in me. That is my fate—a fate I have brought upon myself through the violence I committed against nature, a fate that works its ever more sinister violence upon me. A mere youth I was. As soon as that youth, against the admonitions of all his friends, embraced the soulless bride, such that afterward he himself became soulless, he demanded of himself that he sacrifice his youthful life to her.

By rights my wife should desire to live with us as our mother, as the one who would run the household for us. Her life should be free and poetic. But she has no capacity to accept the grateful trust of a son, and so I will have to shatter all my social ties to her if I am to attain my freedom to act. She is not noble enough to resolve firmly to do anything, and so she is incapable of responding to the rare sort of trust that you too have shown her. The fault lies in her nature: she cannot invest a high and magnificent trust in anyone, because her spirit is entirely lacking in depth. She is deficient in the holiness that conquers the world and defeats fear and death. She will never hold me back. Am I not a man? Am I not proud?

Do not write me any more letters, for she will see to it that they never reach me. Your earlier letters are secure: I have hidden them among some tomes of Greek literature where the nosy woman will never find them. Oh, if only she were either truly grand or unspeakably horrid—in either case I would be saved. But as it is, what can I do with her, she with all her murderous kindness!? As matters stand, two persons are being sacrificed here because neither of them can sacrifice a third person. It is only right that my Karoline has come to her senses—a good spirit warned her. For I now lack the life that could grant her warmth. I am not hard enough to kill—although I can die.

Now it is up to you to want this love of mine. You *should* want it. Regard my words as the onset of my dominion over you, a dominion you yourself desire. I have a talent for domination. I live now in complete separation from Sophie. For the first time, in this new and celibate priesthood, I feel perfectly happy: I am pure in the service of the pure. But I am also proud and commanding. Like a true priest, trusting in the power of prayer to compel his God to perform miracles, so will I compel you to reveal your miracles to me, in order that you and I alike may glory in them.

It remains to be said that several of my friends here still have doubts about you, to wit, whether you have the talents that married life requires and whether your love of me will endure. Because I do not share these doubts, I do my best to confute them. I am happy to report that our friend Daub is entirely on our side. He does think that your poetry shows you to be excessively masculine and rather too bold. Other colleagues of mine wish that you would not pursue that faddish new philosophy. You know that I myself find Schelling to be of an utterly unpoetic nature, and believe me, I know how to dispose of that sort of person.

Apropos of nothing, I spent some time with Arnim recently. His way of behaving does not deviate from that of the usual sort of ethical person. He seems to be clearheaded, and such clarity makes him cheerful, as is the case with Savigny. He cuts a pleasing figure and has a pleasant education behind him, although he is not so blindingly handsome as his portraits make him out to be.

Our relationship is a secret here in Heidelberg, and that is how it will have to remain. But I suppose we must face the fact that your family needs to know something about us. Surely, you won't let them think that all this is my fault? You'll have to be strong, stalwart, and coolly courageous so that your will shall be done. On second thought, should not the legal dispute with your mother—for your paternal inheritance, which she has withheld and which we would need—be settled before we let the world know about us? It is for the sake of secrecy that I am writing this in Greek letters. If you are in touch with Daub or other colleagues, try to convince them that you have the will and the talent to lead a married life. As for Savigny, he seems to have a rather crude conception of my love for you. It would be best not to breathe a word about us to him.

And while we are on the subject of Savigny, I have to say this. During all the years before he saddled himself with a wife, the two of us had clear skies over our heads, and we could talk to one another without needing a translator or mediator. It is clear that since his marriage he can see me only through the distorting glass that others have put into his hands. He has to know what he has sacrificed, namely, a loyal friendship, and for what? I am proud enough to believe that by marrying a Brentano he has entered into a boisterous life, a colorful and hectic life, but not the pious family life he was hoping for. You may communicate to him whatever you like, but do not breathe a word about my relationship with you. You also seem to be still listening to Bettine, even though you concede that she is a hopeless blabbermouth. I call her a coquette. And this entire house, these Brentanos, what have they ever wanted with you other than to rule over you and betray you! The whole problem is that you haven't the courage to break with them. Either rely on yourself and let the houses of Savigny and Brentano go to perdition or at least maintain with them a relation of merely extrinsic convenience. As for me, they no longer exist. Forgive me for tiring you with all these complaints! Don't be angry with me but understand my anger. And tear yourself loose from all these wretched people!

Karoline

Günderrode to Creuzer: Your friends believe that I should stop studying Schelling, and you seem to agree with them. I am grateful to my destiny for having permitted me to live long enough to grasp something of Schelling's divine philosophy and even to have a sense for what I do not yet grasp, grateful at least that before my death the meaning of its heavenly truths has dawned in me. As for my devotion to this new philosophy, how can I apologize for what I take to be the most excellent thing in me? Schelling therefore stays. May we both learn from him in years to come.

Your words about Sophie trouble me. You have allowed your wife to assume proportions that amount to your entire fate, but you brought that particular fate on yourself, and now on us. Yet one should not give oneself over to a fate, claim to honor that fate, and then grumble about it.

And now you have doubts about me as well. Your friends are afraid that I would be unworthy of you if I did not know how to live in a way that accords with their wishes and their circumstances. And so it is, I would indeed be unworthy of you. I am asked whether I have the will and the capability to marry. I know that I would strive eternally to be and to act in the way you desire, in accord with your inmost nature, so that your exterior and interior lives alike would be well-preserved without cares or troubles. I don't know what more to say. My life would justify me, not my words.

As for the need for secrecy, I can only confirm it: the legal battle with my mother makes total secrecy necessary.

With regard to those doubts not only of your friends but of your own, I do not understand this change of heart in you. How often you have told me that my love illuminates and elevates your entire life, and now you find our relationship detrimental to you. How much you would have given earlier on to attain this detriment! But so it is with you all: once attained, the prize is always flawed in your eyes. It seems to me that you are a mariner to whom I have entrusted my entire life. But now storms are brewing, the waves are rising, and the winds carry strange sounds to my ear; I hearken to them and learn that the mariner is taking counsel with his crew as to whether he should toss me overboard or at best abandon me on the shore. You see, that is the position I feel I am in. But my feelings should not decide the matter. If you believe you are in danger, save yourself, put me ashore. No one can blame you, not even I.

The friendship I meant to have with you was a bond for life, a bond unto death. Is that too serious for you? Too irrational? Once upon a time the thought that you would die with me seemed quite valuable to you, along with the thought that if you should die before me you would snatch me down below with you. But now you have much more weighty things on your mind, you believe I might become useful to the world in some way, and then it would be a shame if you were the cause of my demise. I must follow your example now and think precisely as you are thinking, and thus I confess that I do not understand this rationality of yours.—Pardon me, I can feel how overexcited I am; my mode of being must be burdensome to you.

My entire life remains devoted to you, my love, my dear friend. I will always belong to you with such devotion; my love makes no demands on you, yet it lives and dies for you. Love me too, love me forever, my beloved. Allow no time and no relationship to come between us. I could not bear the loss of your love, but I worry about your stamina. You should be more imperious, you should handle me first with love and then with despotism. Never forget, beloved soul, that I am your very own property; never talk to me in any other way.

Promise me you will never leave me. Oh, life of my life, do not abandon my soul. Don't you see, I have become freer and purer since renouncing all our earthly hopes. Panic and pain have dissolved into holy melancholy. Our fate is sealed. Yet you are mine beyond every fate. You can no longer be torn from me since I have won you in this way. May you too find the peace that has blessed me over the past few days, for I love you more fervently, more purely, more blessedly than I ever did when our hopes still blossomed.

Friedrich Creuzer

Creuzer to Günderrode: You accuse me of wavering, but it is the world that is oscillating and even quaking, not I. I am not weak. I have the courage to act and to be long-suffering. You have given me much, perhaps only to deprive me of much. Your letter is proud. I will have to find a way to rescue my own pride. How incorrect is your assertion that whenever the slightest collision occurs I give up on you.

The trust that you showed me during the very first hours of our acquaintanceship was the trust you might have had in an old friend. From the very first moment, however, love poured out of me. Can I say how it came to be? Who can withstand a deity? Yet how did I come to reside in *your* heart? How was I able to warm myself on your chaste bosom? To be sure, I should not brood over such questions after the fact. No interrogations, but only *gratitude*—as though for a gentle gift that a pious soul extends to a thirsting, languishing pilgrim.

Preserve me in your love. Never doubt me. *Qui dubitat, is peccat.* O you beloved and noble creature! eternally joined to me as my spouse! eternally, albeit not by dint of a declaration by some priest! Do not make this mistake about me, beloved angel, do not say I lack courage. Do you not see, it is out of love for you that I am afraid. Can you not feel what it costs me to restrain my feet when they are hastening toward you? how I dream of being in your arms? how I feel the sweet breath of your mouth? how I look into the radiant blue of your eyes? how my nearness to you in dreams mellows me and delights me when I think my head is lying on your breast? Can I ever be happier than in the conviction that the identical longing is devouring the two of us? Lina, Lina, how I love you! O that blessed hour, when may I look upon you! When can I possess my Lina and hold her in my arms and never, never let her go?

You must understand, I need the enjoyments of love—up till now I've experienced more of its pains than its delights. You must understand, I am a young man, and I have had to renounce for a long time now the most splendid things in life.

Now there is no misunderstanding between us. Actually, there never was. Nothing more can separate us other than space and destiny. Other people can no longer divide us.

Yes, you are unhappy, but, truly, not only because of your destiny but even more so on account of your self. What troubles me most is that insistent theme of yours—that you wish to be acquitted of this life, that you would take matters into your own hands and seek the shortest possible route to eternity. The thought that by annihilating your body you would approach eternal life ahead of time, a thought that seems to dominate you, is incorrect according to even the basic principles of the philosophy that is so dear to you. If you are to remain my pupil, then you must follow the counsels of Pythagoras and take reasonable care of your body. I will not stop until you promise me that for as long as you can you will remain in life for both our sakes, since this is the meaning of our entire union, the very meaning of our bond, namely, that we will gladly go only when nature compels us to depart, full of the happy conviction that we will find our love among the shades.

What I wish you most of all is tranquility of soul. *Tranquillum et serenum est oculorum tuorum lumen, tranquilla quoque et serena sit vita tua, tranquillus et serenus animus!* The prevailing climate in your heart of hearts should be such as the poets sing concerning the Blessed Isles: cloudless, halcyon, mildly and gently vitalized by a warm breeze (but not scorched by the noonday heat, which destroys the flowers of your life and the most beautiful blossoms of your spirit). But you must not die, not before me, you my life! *Mea salus Tua salute continentur.*

How very much I am looking forward to our days together in Winkel! O you lovely angel, how good it is that you plan to stay there for such a long time. Set everything up for us, set it up just right, do you hear, Lina! Adieu sweet maid, love of my life, adieu.

Karoline

It took something more than patience to teach Bettine anything. Her imagination was a butterfly or a bird on the wing, but her discipline was a sloth. She was good at history as long as it was entertaining. We drew a detailed map of Odysseus's wanderings after the war at Troy, and she loved chasing across the Mediterranean after him. But give her a philosophy book and you had to be ready for a revolt.

—Your Schelling and your Fichte and your Kant are all impossible churls, superfoetated heads over shriveled hearts! Repulsion, Attraction, Supreme Potency?! I get the repulsion part, but where is the attraction? You need an axe to break into all that jargon. They must have been dropped on their heads when they were children. Tell the truth, don't you find them all horribly arrogant?

—But Schelling is a devoted lover of nature—like you!

—Not at all! If you love nature you lay your head on her breast and you wait and hope for inspiration. A philosopher goes after nature like a lynx after prey. He snatches up some tender morsel and drags it back to his den, where he has a camouflaged factory of concepts, and there he mangles that morsel and feeds it to his underlings. After that, he fine tunes his machinery, adjusts this cog or that weight, showing his adepts how good his system is at mangling things. They believe him—they call his machine a dialectical perpetuum mobile—and afterward, dizzied by its rotations, they are more stupefied than ever.

Bettine was hopeless, so much is true. But I never really gave up on her. At our best, we shared our deepest thoughts about life and death and love. I would have wanted to continue sharing them—until Creuzer declared that she was a mindless flirt and a chatterbox and that she and her brother Clemens would gossip about us and ruin everything. He was adamant. I know I will have to shut her out of my life. Our life, which is now my only life.

Bettine

You said the whole point of living was to come to know lots of things, learn lots of things, and then to die young. Why did you say that? Think about it. It makes no sense. To gather up all that learning—and then drop it all? No. It is not logical. You will laugh to hear me use that word. Go ahead. Laugh! Do!

I live only for you. Do you hear me? I am at my wits' end. I am at the end of my tether. *You* are the great one! You know that, and I know it too. But I dare not tell you so, I know that as well. Anyway, maybe it is not true. You are not so great, not so grand, you are a child, a fragile child, and because you cannot bear the pain you want to say *no* to it all, you want to cast a shroud over everything and not merely whatever it is you think you've lost, you want to throw a pall of oblivion over all the world. But if on this sad Earth you are looking for a place of repose, a place of rest, what do you think my breast and my belly are for?

Whenever I am around you the *world* seems great—not you, the *world*. There is something pure and clean about your life. Because of that purity you pick up all the traces the world has to offer! You take it all in. The world gathers itself in you!

You know you can depend on me. When the abyss gapes before you and threatens to swallow you, drop everything and come to me. We'll go down together, no path is gloomy if you walk it with me, I love the dark, dear Günderrode!—I know how impatient my letters have made you, they are so silly and self-absorbed, they are the squeals of a child chasing soap bubbles, performing cartwheels and card tricks for the grownups. But I swear to you I am not self-absorbed, I am not showing off, however silly I seem. I am not Narcissus. I am Echo. I never wanted to find myself. I wanted to find *you*.

But I felt it in your last letter to me. You want to pull away from me. You want to shut me out. You are withdrawing from me. My pen stops, it won't touch the paper, it won't let me write these things. I did not say them. No. It isn't true.

Karoline

I must put you out of my life, Bettine darling, I must banish you, shut you out, expel you. Creuzer insists on it, and he is now my entire life—all of it, the last drop of it. It is less about you than about Clemens. Creuzer fears your brother's caustic, and he is frightfully jealous of Clemens. I once thought I might enjoy igniting a man's jealousy. But there is no joy in it. It is a mean, vulgar trait. I hope to expunge it from Creuzer's character as from my own. Till then, you and your brother must go.

It is not like me to act so decisively. It is not like me to act at all. Loving is laborious. It demands actions beyond our capability. It exhausts me, defeats me. Whereas you, for all your talk of passivity, hold intercourse with the stars of the sky, boldly compelling them to reply to your queries, I would sooner acquiesce in their pale radiance as a child acquiesces in the gentle rocking of the cradle. You feel compelled to do battle with all the world, and it seems you were given the mettle to do so. You have seen that my situation is quite different. I hope that in your future some congenial force will flow together with your own, so that at least for a moment you can retire from battle.

I suppose the riddle that will be put to us both is whether the life we have lived was worth the labor.—Plans are so easily frustrated; better therefore not to make any. Best is to be ready for all the eventualities that may promote what is worthiest in us, so that we can do the one thing, the single thing we are obliged to do. And what is that? Never to wound the holy principles that planted themselves in the soil of our deepest convictions, to develop these principles further by our actions and our beliefs, so that in the end we can do nothing other than confess that which from the origin is divine in us. The noblest school of life seems to me the one that tells us never to deny, neither in spirit nor in action, those basic principles, the ones that consecrate our innermost essence. That school does not release the noble human being until he breathes out the last breath of his life. I also think that the supreme mark of excellence in a destiny is that one be prodded by ever more stringent tests.

Of course, we are women, not men. If we cannot be heroes, then we must bear heroes. The time is not yet propitious for us. There are times

114

of ebb and times of flood, and our time is at ebb tide. All now is mere preparation, to awaken a feeling, to exercise our forces and gather them up so they may grasp a higher potency of spirit. Why should we not admit that the whole point of our lives is development, a continuous unfolding? For our destiny is the mother that bears fruit, the fruit of the ideal, beneath her heart.—

Goethe

Principles and ideals—yes, of course we need them, lest the world fall into the hands of the unprincipled cynic, the diplomat and the mean merchant, the courtier and courtesan, the hired assassin. The problem is whether and when those principles and ideals, by virtue of their severity and unforgiving nature, subvert the life they are meant to nurture. There is something acidic about principled righteousness. It is as though the metal hoops the cooper applies to the oaken staves to keep the barrel intact eat away at the wood until the joinings gape or the bottom gives way altogether and the wine is spilled on the ground. We are invariably surprised by such sudden failures, such breaches, although they happen so often that we ought to have become wise to the danger. To add to it all, corrosion and collapse happen in our very best persons, in our hardest and sweetest wood, and still we are baffled, and we learn nothing.

How many times in my life, especially in my travels, have I had greater faith in a rascal than in the man of principle. A rascal has less corrosive cruelty about him; he desires only his advantage, not my life. In the end, Mephistopheles is but a rascal. The truly subversive spirit of severe and unrelenting ideals lies in some higher or deeper sphere than his. And that would be the murderous sphere, the killing sphere, even if it drapes itself in the robes of righteousness and right. For those robes too are black as night.

Bonaventura

And still I eavesdrop at the windows and in the doorways of the village houses. The good and the just are exhorting the poor mortals within to lead a principled life and to die a principled death. I listen for the nine key words that are sure to fall. A cat has nine lives, and nine are the principal words of a principled life and death. Ah, there falls the first—duty! followed soon by the second—obligation! and on its heels falls the third—responsibility! How familiar the dirge is! But there is more to come.

My ears are pricked for the maxims of the good and the just and the unforgiving. My ears have not long to wait. Conscience! Conviction! Confession! I nearly fall to my knees, called upon to submit utterly to the compulsory vocabulary. Only a few items are missing now. Wait. Wait for just a moment. For they are bound to fall, as spring rain and winter snow are bound to fall. Selflessness! Surrender! Sacrifice!—all pronounced with the hissss of the serpent!

These are the nine nails, the nine flesh-wounding hooks and barbs of the cat-o'-nine-tails of the modern heart. And the scourge is wielded by the hand that conducts the principled life. Miraculously, the hand that operates the cat-o'-nine-tails of the Hyperborean heart and applies it to your naked back is no one's hand but your own! It is as though you yourself dreamed up this horror! Yet it was not you. It was the machination of princes and priests—in one word, of the police.

Where have the ancient wisdoms gone? What has happened to the sages of old? Do they languish in the dungeons of the unforgiving? And their sage words—are they drowned out by the caterwauling of us mortifying moderns?

Heraclitus of Ephesus

I sit on the steps of the temple of Artemis and I watch the children play. The children rule. We are so devoted to them because their rearing is so uncertain a thing, so haphazard in its outcome. They are our kings, we their slaves.

A young woman walks by. She too seems a child to me, although she is marvelously grown. Her look has the intensity of a child at play, although she is not playing. Life is a tautly strung bow, and the arrow's notch is fitted tight to the bowstring, ready to fly. Lifedeath is the bow. There is melancholy in the woman's look. Impulsive too she seems to me. Some god is at work in her. Dionysos, perhaps, or Hades—though these two are one and the same, the way up is the way down, all is approach. She disappears in the glare of the afternoon sun.

Lightningbolt is but sudden sun, and it steers all things. The sun only seems to set, it is never-setting, and there is nowhere to hide. Does it sink into the sea? Do you hear a hiss? No, the first of fire's tropes is the sea, for the sun causes the sea to exhale water as cloud, cloud rains to rivers, rivers run to the sea, and so it goes, measure by measure, a ringdance or circledance, sunlight and lightningbolt governing all, apportioning by lays or lots. And no difference makes a difference in the end, since all is unending differencing, even the difference between mortals and immortals, which comes to naught. The mysteries are right about this: the mortals are forever undying and the immortals are forever dying; each lives the death of the other and dies the other's life. The muses deliver the Delphic sign and the mortals are bemused. The tension may be not that of the bow after all but of the poet's lyre, plucked and strummed in accord with the grand rhythm, the sole song that must be sung.

No one here understands anything of this. They are all too busy. No intensity, only hectic indecision. They are like jackasses, frantically undecided, scurrying between two equidistant haystacks; they hurry back and forth between them, starving themselves, unable to act. Perhaps she understood, that intense one, that melancholy one passing by: day night, winter summer, war peace, satiety hunger—this is god, this is the concealed harmony, so much more powerful than the evident cacophony, and nature does love to play hide-and-seek, as these children do. Fire smells like what you toss onto it, so that if everything went up in smoke we could follow our noses to the truth. But not smoke, fire is the thing. The cosmos, the one and only world, created by neither gods nor humans, always was and is and will be ever-living fire, igniting and extinguishing in rhythmic turns. If you can step into that rhythmic circledance and follow its tact, if you can discern the apportioned lays or lots, if you can gather together what is lying right there in front of you and let it lie right there in front of you, well then, you do not need to listen to me, and I do not need to listen to you.

The children at play and that melancholy beauty passing in the glare of the sun have my full attention as evening turns in tact to night.

> Ephesus surrenders itself to slumber,
> Stretching across nocturnal Panormos;
> Motley life subsides in city lanes,
> Clouds of night encircle the moon.
> In a night sky bedecked with stars,
> Heraclitus alone stops and stares;
> Thoughts encircle his brow.

Empedocles of Acragas

Splendid singer, it was a god who closed your eyes.
Yet with thinking eyes you still behold
The cosmic cornucopia.

I speak with forkèd tongue, it seems, and yet forsooth
Each tine of mine, each word and phrase, will prick a truth
That hides itself from prying mortal eyes. My tongue
Conforms itself to double truth, for this One Sphere
Contains two kinds of force that strive within the whole.
Though one whose name is Strife now lends the whole its name,
The other force, which we call Love, will rise to tame
Dispute and cause. For Love and Strife, each one in turn,
Will rule the roots of being and steer the fourfold all
Within the Sphere: the sun, our golden glistening Zeus,
And Hera, bearing in her bosom all that lives,
Aidoneus, Hades, god of earth and underworld,
And Nestis, weeping cloud, life-giving rain and dew.
In times of Strife these four will tangle, all in rage,
In times of Love they kiss, embrace, at peace and sage
In all their deeds and all their proclamations.
Yet once they've grown together by dint of mighty Love,
Keen Strife usurps the center, the fourfold flies apart,
Anarchic are such times as these, sons scorn their sires,
And sires strike their sons. Contention and commotion
Hold sway, and people show how stupid they can be,
How careless and how reckless now of life and limb
And Love.

•

You see how we have lapsed, how Strife is everywhere
On these our plains of doom, our cities of decline.
You see how we must live, your heart is so enraged

120

You cannot think. For thought is not of head but heart;
To think is but to bathe in all-supporting seas
Of blood that flow about the core. Pericardial
Is thought, pericardial in times of peace, when Love
Regains the center. Look! you see her rise already,
Kypris Aphrodite! You hear her call to you,
"Come to me, you weary ragged mortal, lie down
Beside me. Know delight again, and laughter, learn
The sense of what it means to be alive at all,
Together, not apart in hate, but all embraced
In harmony."

•

If you should ask me how I know these things, then I
Must tell you not a double tale but multiple,
A forkèd tongue would not suffice to say them all.
I learned by leading many lives. A boy I was,
As you may well believe, but a girl too I was,
That melancholy girl passing there, so singular
And so intense, was I myself, when Love ruled in
The Sphere. That bird in the bush you see was me,
The bush itself was I myself, and look! that
Flying fish a-leap, the brine now flashing golden on
Its scales—all these things that you perceive to be
I was. Yet much of what I saw I ate, I drew
Blood, I slaughtered, I lived an unholy life,
And so I wander here a fugitive, a child,
Forlorn and destitute, of unremitting Strife.

•

I climb the lavascape, the crater gapes below.
I hear the call to heroism and to sacrifice.
I am the one they call. But then a voice, afar:
"Are you the one? are you this? are you so sure
Of what you see? of who you are? have you the right
To take the shortest route from here to timelessness?"
I falter. I am unsure. The distant voice assails me:

"Put not your trust in Strife, but in a better time
To come. The reign of Love will soon recur,
Never ending, ever changing, as indeed it must.
Put not your faith in quarrel and in raging Strife,
But calm your turbulence—and sheathe your knife."

Karoline

And yet my mood is leaden. It is more than the usual torpor. Nothing brings me joy, even if nothing in particular is painful to me. At such moments I am in the most wretched state, that of feeling nothing at all, and the dull and dark despond drags on. It is not anxiety. It is the feeling that I cannot get a hold on anything, everything slips away into nothingness, taking me with it. I am at home nowhere; everything around me is indifferent. The world has lost its hold on me. When I feel that condition coming on, I hate myself. But it does come.

I feel the life force draining out of me, liquid love evaporating. When Creuzer trembles, grows rigid, cries out the name of God, whimpers and collapses, he drains the life force into me. He sleeps, his labors accomplished. I feel the full weight of him on me and in me. It is not his child that I carry; *he* is the child I carry. Then I feel his life force too draining out of me. I will gather up the sheets in the morning after he departs. He will swear eternal love as he always does before going out the door.

Does nothing endure? Is it all drainage, efflux of influx, effluvium and stain? All that exertion, the labor of love, no doubt, but accomplishing what? Is there no monument to excellence? Nothing set in stone but only stony silence?

When Creuzer says how soft my breasts are and how he wishes his heavy head would never have to quit those cushions, I have to think of Clemens, my naughty boy. Creuzer hates Clemens with a passion, but that is because Clemens holds a mirror up to him. They are both figures out of Clemens' *Godwi: The Stony Image of the Mother*. These orphans need the softness of my breasts. They need the warmth of my underbelly, and the wet, their souls are so cold, so desiccated. They do not need the rest of me, which is cut from a quarry. My dear Hölderlin says it best: *As my sky is of iron, so I am of stone.* And once again the poet cries out, and his cry is my own: *Oh, Bellarmine, where have all our friends gone?*

The Surgeon

She was engaged in research on behalf of Professor Creuzer in Heidelberg, research on the life and death of Marcus Junius Brutus. Or so she told me. Of course I found it odd that a woman would be meddling in university research. More than odd. Even so, she was a timid thing and, in her own way, quietly convincing. How could I have known? She spoke more hurriedly once she had my ear, saying that after losing the second battle at Philippi, Brutus fell on his sword.

—But what does that mean? she asked. Did he simply fall? How did he arrange the sword? And how could he know that the wound would be fatal?

I had to confess that the precise manner and cause of Brutus's death were unknown to me. I had more recent cases to occupy me. One could only surmise. I did speculate, however. One has to be of assistance. Never disappoint a lady.

—He must have seen to it that the sword would penetrate his heart. He must have calculated the precise point and the exact angle of entry. Otherwise he would merely have hurt his pride.

—But all those bones—a fortress of ribs! The heart is so well protected!

—Ah, yes, a mighty fortress is our heart—but with walls that can be breached, never fear. If you know your anatomy!

It is difficult to satisfy an inquisitive student. Yet one must try. Knowledge is ever a good, ignorance ever a blight on the good. I explained that in every higher mammal the bulk of the heart is shielded by the septum, but that in humans the left ventricle is not. It obtrudes to the left, as though peeking around the corner of the breastbone.

—If one turns the blade to the horizontal, to avoid its being caught in the ribs, entry is in the end not so difficult. The fascia, the pectoral muscles major and minor, even the pericardial sac—none of these nor all of them together would be a match for a sword entering at the proper angle. Or for that matter a rapier, a poignard, or a dagger of any decent size.

—Decent size? Proper angle?

—A mere four inches to the heart, I said.

As for the proper angle, that was more difficult to explain. I showed her on Fritz, my office skeleton, who always comes in handy in situations like this. Without intending it or quite realizing it, I was offering her an advanced seminar in anatomy. I must say she was an apt pupil.

—From the top of his left ribcage, I explained, Brutus would have counted down to the fourth and fifth ribs; the space between them would be the point of attack.

—And the angle of the thrust?

—Upward at no more than forty-five degrees.

She shuddered. But then she did something that astonished me. With both hands she searched for her top rib through her white blouse, her fingers then probing on the descent. She soon gave up.

—It seems one solid mass to me! How was he ever able to count?

I smiled.

—It would have been easier had he undressed. And much easier had he been a woman. Normally the space between the fourth and fifth rib is where the breast terminates.

—Terminates?

I elaborated. Not to the point of indelicacy, I trust.

—Not where it ends, exactly, but at the lower line of its attachment to the torso—where the line of shadow begins, as it were.

—The line of shadow, she repeated, somewhat dreamily it seemed to me.

—The line of shadow, I confirmed.

A pause.

—And then what happens? she said.

My look must have betrayed some measure of doubt, perhaps suspicion, perhaps even worry. Her voice became more assertive.

—I mean, how long did it take for Brutus to die?

—Why do you wish to know?

—He is reported to have uttered some last words. Professor Creuzer and I worry about the authenticity of this.

—As well you might. Unless he uttered them before he fell on that sword. There are two scenarios. His heart may have continued pumping, filling the pericardial sac with blood until the heart suffocated and drowned, as it were. He might have remained conscious for a few moments. But those moments would have been confused. It is unlikely he would have made speeches.

—And the second scenario?

—If the sword actually penetrated the left ventricle, the heart would most likely have fibrillated—as though in seizure or convulsion, no longer pumping blood but frozen in a death grip, as it were. The brain needs a steady flow of blood. He would have swooned almost immediately. Again, no speeches.

—At least the pain would stop, she said absently.

—Death stops everything, I replied.

After she left my consultation room, I reflected that it had been one of oddest interviews I'd ever had. Not even in the surgical theater did I get such insistent and intelligent interrogations.

Some time in August, the report of her death reached me. I felt betrayed. Perhaps Caesar crossed my mind. He too was betrayed.

—*Et tu, Brute.*

IV

Karoline

Weariness. Already in the mornings, when I used to feel fresh and ready to write, I feel exhausted, as though after a long day's reading. I feel now that my time is winding down, that my continuing to live is merely an error on nature's part. Why does my heart not do the right thing? Why does it not simply surrender? Why does it resist the conclusion of the syllogism? What was all that study for, if not for drawing conclusions like strings to close a sack? At times this feeling of weariness paralyzes me; at other times the feeling loosens its grip. When it relents, I stumble on. That is my résumé.

My eyelids are red and swollen all the time now from reading and weeping. And those spots of gray and black in my field of vision—vitreous opacity, says the physician. Glass covered with black tar. Or the silver tain of a mirror tarnished and scratched. Whatever it is, the eyes deteriorate day by day, so that I can scarcely see the image in my psychè. It is as though these spots are expanding: one day they will swallow the world whole in the blackness of darkness. That will take time, no doubt. The migraines will work faster. I will waken one morning with a cracked skull, my brain cradled in the pillow.

Sometimes I have the feeling that I am standing next to my own coffin, staring down at my own dead body, studying the corpse. That is the way I looked at Charlotte in the end, but now Charlotte is Karoline. My own dead body? My cadaver? That is also the feeling I have when I read what I have written the day before.

I splash water on my face. I struggle to be lucid. But lucidity too is oppressive, bound up with a thousand painful memories; it cannot forget that it is imprisoned in time, manacled to earth and temporality. Lucidity therefore knows nothing of eternity. Eternity lies in dreams. There, in dreams, time's calculus counts for nothing. Blessed contentment lies in dreams, and it is only such blessed contentment that we dream of.—We withdraw into ourselves and weave a world that is ours alone. Airy visions inflate us, our souls begin to levitate. This is how I imagine it must be for one who is expiring: awareness grows weak and intermittent, the oneiric cloak wraps the dying one round, dreams marry figures of reality until reality disappears and the dreamer becomes the dream. And in that dream I can pace across all the centuries of time and all the reaches of space to engage in sweet conversation with anyone I like, with all my friends from afar.

Zarduscht

Many die too late; some too early. My teaching may strike you as strange, O my brothers and sisters, but it is the most important lesson to be learned in life: die at the right time.

To have outlived one's time, to hang on stubbornly to the tree of life like a piece of overripe, wrinkled fruit, to procrastinate for no earthly reason—what greater humiliation can there be? To be all too zealous about ending it all, to deprive the world of the things one could have accomplished—what greater loss can there be? It is difficult to get our dying right.

To be sure, if one has never *lived* at the right time, one will never understand my teaching. Better that such a one never had been born. Better that such a one had attended the school of Silenos the Satyr. Silenos says that the best thing for mortals, women as well as men, is—never to have been born. But once one has been born, the second best is—to die as soon as you can. That teaching, my friends, potent as it is, is not my teaching. Be not precipitous! But also: be not a laggard.

I teach a free death. Not that death is without cost—its cost is infinite. But free in the sense that I *will* my death, will it *freely* and without reserve. Not that I merely capitulate to the inevitable, but that I sink my teeth into inevitability and bite.

A free death is not a suicide. Nor does it accept Silenos's claim that the tiniest coffin is best. One must learn to make one's death a celebration of life, and timing is the key to every rite of celebration. Not too late, but not too early. Not the endless road, but also not the shortcut. Not to insult the Earth's hospitality by insisting on staying, but also not to offend her by beating a hasty and ungrateful retreat.

To be free in one's dying is to be a holy naysayer when the time to say yes has elapsed. That your dying blaspheme neither your life nor the Earth, my brothers and sisters, that is my plea to the honey of your souls. May your dying glow in your matutinal spirit and in your midday virtue; may it blaze as the colors of eventide spread over the Earth's horizon for your sake. Otherwise your death will not have gone well.

I myself want to die now, at this instant of exultation—let this be the instant of my death!—so that you, my friends, will love the Earth all the more for my sake. And I want to become earth myself once again, returning to the stillness that gave birth to me. I had my turn at the game, I had my goals and my dreams, and now I want to toss the golden ball to you who inherit my goals and my dreams.

More than anything else, O my brothers and sisters, I want to withdraw a while and watch you play the game.—Yet watching you is not dying but living on. I have to smile. Evidently, I linger a while longer on this Earth. Forgive my malingering! Evidently, this is not the instant of my death. I procrastinate. I postpone.

—Thus confessed Zarduscht.—

Karoline

After Eusebio—neither Odysseus nor his son Telemachos—in visit after visit began to fill her, Calypso—yes, it was Calypso, the hidden one, and no one else—dropped her hunting lance and began to check her calendar. What if she were pregnant with his child? That would make her happy. Even if they could never marry, so that the child would be born in shame, as the world calls it, the fatherless child would fill her life. And even if the child inherited all his traits, she would still love it and nurture it with her own milk. And when the time came that the child needed more than her breast, she would find money somewhere, somehow, through some form of heroic sacrifice.

That is how I would have written the story.

By that time, by the time a child might have been underway, the courts would surely have restored my paternal inheritance to me. Father would bless my using it to raise his grandchild. I would read to the child perched on my lap, as my father read to me. I would read to her or him a whole library of good books.

And so I wrote to Eusebio to say that I would be proud to bear his children. He replied that he was deeply honored—but would it not be wiser for me to have them with someone else? He mentioned two possible progenitors that he felt might be currently amenable. They at least could give the bastard a surname and supply the cash for its wants.

My belly shrank as I read the letter. Had I been pregnant, the fetus would have been crushed.

Eusebio means piety. But is piety pusillanimity? Does it all come down to cowardice? And is this what I, the creator of fabulous heroines who are prepared to love unto death, ready to leap into the flames as the Malabrian widows of India do, or to die in battle or in childbirth, as fate decrees, have won to myself? Piety?

Not even that.

It is evening. Lamps are being lit in the houses all about, from the riverbank all the way up to the vineyards. Only the blackbird sings. The rest is silence.

Friedrich Creuzer

She is exhausting me. She is draining the life force out of me. I cannot stay away from her, I run to her like a starving animal. It is an illness, an epidemic, an addiction. When I am not with her I am stretched out with longing, my limbs languish, my ligaments and tendons melt, my mouth goes dry; when I am with her I am stretched out in another way, I sprawl like a dog in the sun, my mouth will not stop. I whimper and I suck.

Whenever I return home to Heidelberg I discover that the Benefactress has transformed into Bovinity, and I hate the very person who orders my life, I hate her with all my soul. I cannot go on this way. I need to lead a well-ordered life. I have my research. I have my students. And I have colleagues who examine me quite closely, unforgiving colleagues.

I hear the Siren call of the nymph who dwells in the humid cave, but that means I am Attis, and the bovine Benefactress will send her lions to tear me apart. The lions will carry the mutilated pieces of me back to her, and she will confront me with her aggrieved looks and silent accusations.

Who is to blame? Daub says it is I alone who am to blame. But I am merely meat in the claws of the Bacchae. They shook my tree. I plummeted. They are devouring me now. I shudder before Agaue, the mother of Pentheus. My name is Grief. No one can save me—not even the nymph of the cave, my Dido, my Circe, my Calypso and Apocalypse, my long-legged, amorous, high-breasted nippled ewer, she of the infinite deep, not even she can save me, especially not she.

Whichever way I wend, there is no escape. It is my Ἄτη, my Doom. I feel my strength waning. My health is under attack. I fear I may collapse. Enough!

Karoline

At times the spleen in me rises and fills me to the full, and I feel I want to write him a different sort of letter, the sort of letter that will scorch his eyes. What sorts of things would I write, what kind of gall would spill onto the page? I would tell him about the three other boys in my life—Achim, my beautiful boy, Savigny, my good boy, Clemens, my naughty boy—and about him, Creuzer, my ugly boy. He is so sensitive about his ugliness, he never stops writing about it, it is in every epistle he pens, even if he never dares to go into detail. I would go into detail, into loving detail concerning his lantern jaw—if in fact it held a lantern it would illumine the world—his ungenerous mouth, lipless, downturned at the corners—it would smile upon the world if the world were standing on its head—his own head far too large for his spavined torso, shoulderless and stooped from all those hours spent over his books, *our* books, the back not quite hunched in a hump but tending that way, his witch's fingers tracing a line across the printed page, the nails far too long and never quite clean enough—a perfect head and body for some distant and as yet undiscovered planet, splendid for some world not yet conceived. As for those other trifles of nature concerning his person, no need to mention them, no need to wield the dagger.

Which gives me a giddy idea, a wicked idea, a splendid idea. I take my kerchief from its place inside my chemise over my heart. Slipping free of my dress and the chemise, I take my dagger and make a small incision over my heart. An exquisite singing sensation on the skin. A rivulet of blood is surprised, and it in turn surprises me. Before it can flow freely, I press my kerchief to the wound, turning its deep white a high red. I will send it to him in a letter. What shall I write?

—I am sending you a kerchief that should be no less significant than the one Othello gave to Desdemona.

Of course, that kerchief was of dire significance for them both, thanks to Iago. And who is Creuzer's Iago? I wonder whether Othello and Iago can be conjoined in one personality. That thought gives me pause. And Desdemona? *Deisidaimonia*? Dispel the demons? Yes, that is what I am about, with dagger and pen, dispelling the demons. How shall I continue my letter?

—I had worn the kerchief over my heart for some time, to consecrate it. I then opened my left breast exactly over the heart, gathering the droplets of blood in its folds. You see how I was able to wound the tenderest part of me for your sake. Press it to your lips; it is my heart's blood! Consecrated in this way, the kerchief will have the rare virtue of preserving you from all dejection and doubt. Furthermore, it will be for you a tender forfeit.

I will enclose a generous lock of my hair, and I will see to it that the missive exudes the ineradicable scent of me. The hair would continue to grow, and the scent would crowd him ever closer.

—Let my hair cascade over your poor frame, my darling, let my atmosphere absorb all your oxygen. Focus not on your ugliness but on your aloneness and your desiccation, slow but steady, as you pore over your books, *our* books, and muse on the co-author you have betrayed and who is now nowhere to be found.

These galling thoughts endure for the time it takes to write them down, and they are still here, knotted inside me like a cyst. I am left to wonder where my Hyperion is, the beautiful boy and the good boy combined, the one who anoints me with the balsam of his love and who knows how to receive my love without being terrified. Together we would advance to the forefront. That is our only obligation. To advance to the forefront like Titans, two Titans, hand in hand. *No one can bear life alone.*

Sophie Creuzer

I will copy out her intercepted letter to him and then I will burn her hair and the blood-stained kerchief and the galling letter, I will burn all of it. It will raise a horrid stench—hair always does that—but I will breathe it in with gratitude and I will count my blessings. Nothing now will come between us. If he gets tempted again—she was so beautiful, so gentle, so pleasing in every way, such a gifted pupil, it made perfect sense to him, I can see that, I can accept that, I was more like a mother to him, I still am very much like a mother to him—all I will have to do is recite the letter to him. He will recognize her voice behind my own, and he will collapse in shame. And I will restore him to health once again as I dependably do.

My thirteen years in excess of him give me a certain advantage. Of course, I may well pass before he does because of that. But afterward he may do as he likes, it will not matter, the advantage will still be mine. He has all the ignorance of innocence and all the insight of guilt. And I have learned how important it is to be a benefactress. She needed me to forgive her, to forgive them both, and it was easy for me to forgive her, for all her condescension and overbearing sympathy, easy because I knew that even though I was the damaged third party I would prevail in the end. Men need good order more than adventure, stability more than titillation, three meals a day and a nurse when they fall ill, it is as simple as that.

Hurry, finish copying. Why does she have to use such big words? I know full well what she means, and so would he have understood had I not intercepted the letter, you don't need such complicated words unless you are trying to hide something. As for me, I was absolutely forthright with her. I told her that to the degree that tranquility would be restored to my husband's life, the tranquility that he formerly possessed in full measure, to that degree my love of her and my friendship to her would extend.

Hurry with the copying now, you have more important things to do. Today is market day, and there is not a potato in the house.

Carl Daub

No one can teach me a thing about the Golgotha of marriage. I understand as well as anyone the crown of thorns, the cross, the nails, and the lance. I understand the tedious days, the slow suffocation. The delusion is to think there can be anything else, that we can find another Eve, a pristine companion who will lead us back to Paradise. There is no other Eve than the one the serpent poisoned back in the beginning once and for all, no other Eve than Lilith. Creuzer was laboring under the illusion that he had found the prelapsarian Eve, and the noxious delusion corrupted his body and baffled his soul. Creuzer has now recovered sufficiently from the nerve fever that drove him to death's door, recovered enough to renounce solemnly his relationship with Günderrode. It is high time; it is time to act. I must inform her of his decision immediately. Creuzer's soul has been before God and continues to lie prostrate before the face of the terrible Father. Only through the aid of His divine Son will that soul be restored.

She will be disappointed, of course. Creuzer is a catch, even with his galling marriage and his deformities. I must be careful not to destroy utterly the object of his misplaced affection: my spouse, a close friend of hers since childhood, would never forgive me, and Christian charity forbids it, no matter how grave her sin, no matter how unworthily she has used him, and prudence is one of the essential virtues. One must practice circumspection. One must exercise caution and discretion in such delicate affairs.

Therefore, a stratagem. I will instruct Susanne von Heyden to write the letter Creuzer has asked me to write—since he cannot bring himself to write it—but I will not have our letters sent directly to Günderrode. Von Heyden will address the packet to the two Servière sisters whom Günderrode is visiting at Winkel. Not the gadabout Brentanos, who are also at Winkel and who have just bought a property there, but the Servières, who, unlike the Brentanos, will also practice prudence. They will report the letters' contents to her, and in no uncertain terms, allowing her no doubt about Creuzer's resolve, yet knowing how to buffer the blow. Not for all the world would I cast a pall over the girl's existence, which of course would be scarcely avoidable if I, a man, were to make the revelation to her myself. For she would then taste the full bitterness of the chalice. I bear nothing but good will toward her, if not toward her sin, and I will act in a way that will surely protect her.

Nevertheless, favoring candor over excessive prudence, and acknowledging that discretion is but the virtue of vile diplomacy, I will see to it that my letter dashes every possible hope and eradicates every possible misconception she may be entertaining: Creuzer has abjured once and for all every possible relationship with her and he urges her to amend her life by returning to God through the grace of His crucified Son whose aid does not fail even the most obdurate sinner.

It is all for the best. She will understand. She will rise to the occasion.

Karoline

Every day I run to meet the postman here in Winkel. By now he smiles knowingly when he sees me coming. Every day he gives me the mail for Paula and Lotte and Herr Mertens.

One of the envelopes, the heaviest one, has a seal I do not recognize. I do not recognize the handwriting of the person who is sending a little packet to Fräulein Charlotte Servière in Winkel; it is certainly not Creuzer's hand, not the hand of my Eusebio, and why would he be writing her anyway and not me? All capitals, the letters of the address, as though written by a school child, or someone pretending to be a child. I love mysteries. I hurry back to the Zehnthof courtyard, leave the rest of the mail on a tea table there, and dash up the stairs to my room with my purloined prize.

Close the door. Lean against it.

Open the envelope carefully, do not tear it.

Take a breath. Lower the heart rate.

Three letters inside, not merely one, a windfall.

None of them addressed to me. But they are all about me.

Uncertainties are now certainties. They race through my bloodstream like the liquor of a viper's bite. One is a sweet missive from my dear Susanne to Charlotte, begging her to mitigate the blow; the others are from friend Daub, who delivers the blow. Daub? I have written him so many times in recent months. I trust him implicitly. I have known both him and his wife since I was a child. He is a man of God.

And yet.

I have lost the tenderest of tender forfeits, it seems. It seems I have lost my love. Through my own stupidity I have lost it. Through Eusebio's stupidity as well, perhaps. But I must pay the full cost of the forfeit. A pact is a pact.

What's in a letter? What's in all the letters of my life? All those spilled words. Here, in these two from Daub to Susanne, a steady stream of lethal words. The words say that I have turned my lover into a sick man. It seems I have turned him into a coward as well. Sick men recover.

How many weeks has it been since I last wrote Eusebio? *I do not understand this change of heart in you.* Should I answer these letters? Does civility require it? To whom could I send them? I am not the addressee. I do not exist.

I look out my window toward the river and the declining sun. A wind stirs, the willows wave. Evening will fall soon. And the night. Let me write a few things down quickly, the things on my mind, bread for the school children, then take a walk.

I suppose it is a grave fault to open someone else's mail. I believe it is also against the law.

The White Slippers

We go trippingly down the wooden stairs of Mertens' lovely Zehnthof, admiring the fancy wooden lattice work and the Provençal blue trim of the white plaster walls. We tell Lotte Servière we're out for a stroll and we set off, slipping out the garden gate at the rear of the courtyard, heading west down the sandy path, wildflowers everywhere. Perhaps we are going to the Brentano house, the delightful domicile the family has just purchased on Plane Tree Way—but no, we have nothing to do with that family, not anymore. We're at Harvester Lane now, and we turn left, crossing Main Street and heading south on White Lane. White Lane is entirely familiar to us, it is our namesake if we may say so, we could walk it blindfolded. Down closer to the river White Lane becomes a sandy path that wends its way between fields of barley and oats now hip high. The sun is low in the sky, but the warmth of the July day lingers. This path too is dry, no dew by now on the grasses and grains. We are heading west again, avoiding the river's edge but walking parallel to it. Apparently we intend to leave the village of Winkel on Rhine behind us, at least for a spell. We approach the hamlet of Bartholomaeus and the line of picturesque grain mills along Magpie Brook. All is well. Life is good.

A mild wind rises to meet us out of the south and west, a mere breeze, a faint trace of atmosphere. But we recognize it. We are alert. More will come. That stirring in the willows to our left, that slight turbulence in the occasional elderberry replete with chattering birds, then a sudden sweep of damp air, that unmistakable trace of odoriferous atmosphere: the river is too close, and the wind is rising. It likes us not.

A river is but the elongated accumulation of rainfall resulting from the compression of infinite time to bounded space. It is a proud and pompous puddle that has gotten too big for its bridges, if we may say so, too vast for its banks, and has overflowed and flooded the land. It is a common enough phenomenon. There are many such rivers, the world a network of waterways, a skein, a web of rivers. Even so, we do not like it, and it does not like us.

Rivers are like Titans, rough gods from a savage age, a holdover from a bygone time, an atavism, a barbarism. They always flow downhill. Where are the ups and downs of heel and toe leading her now? We shall exert our collective will to the fullest and steer her to safety, to dry soles and many happy returns. Yet our willpower does not suffice. We cannot turn her aside. As always, alas, we are forced to conform.

But what is this? Three old men in antique costume approach. Friends! Old friends! We recognize them. The oldest, in the forefront, strides in high-heeled black leather Persian boots—and in this heat! But a mind like his pays no heed to the weather. Behind him, for the path is narrow, an Ionian Greek in Lydian sandals, leatherwork like lace, delicate yet durable. We recognize him as the man of paradoxes. And, bringing up the rear, his shoeless fugitive feet having borne him all the way from seabound Sicily, the lover of Love and the victim of Strife, the man who spins in the vortex. Friends! Companions in arms!

They are upon us. She will stop and exchange pleasantries with them. But no. We do not pause to pass the time of day. She walks on by without a word. We see them raise a hand in some antique salute, χαίρετε, hailand-farewell, hellogoodbye. We march in solemn procession until we arrive at the place where the brook runs into the hated river.

Already the willows overhead are weeping. Their web of weedy branches veils the sky, their lachrymose, elongated leaves sway and sob in the wind. The elderberry bushes are moribund, their moss-covered wood gone spongy. Half the branches are already dead; the startled birds have flown. One distant blackbird, or perhaps a nightingale or a thrush, we hear. The sand of the riverbank is no longer the amiable sand of the paths we have left behind.

Something is afoot. Our straw dampens. We are too close. We are on the edge. She gathers stones together. To every season there is a purpose. The wind is up, begins to whirl and moan. She removes some thing from the bosom of her red dress, some thing that glistens in the slanting sun. We close our eyelids.

The Rhine

Much remains murky. Farther out, where by day and by night barges glide by, I flow more freely and there is greater clarity. But close to the banks on either side of me, my waters are turbid. Grasses grow, willows shed their leaves and their limbs, the towns and cities of countless persons release their effluvium into me.

There are looks that tell you nothing, gazes that glaze over, eyes that grant you no entry. You are uncertain whether anything registers in those eyes, whether anything of the world is received or read.

She gazes blankly on the surrounding hills, and blankly she looks into me. I have seen that look before, both from others and from her. The vacant look. The long look that is never long enough.

> In proud arcs and then in gentle curves
> I pour my waters, I, the royal river Rhine.
> Through valleys then I flow, on by the rocks,
> As the hills around me gaze into my flood.
> They see their hilltops veiled in greenish moss
> And are astonished by their own monstrous shape.
> Narcissus was so pleased to stare into the flood,
> Seeing reflected there his perfect physiognomy.
> He could not turn away. The peaks about me
> Do not share the joy he felt in that sweet face of his.
> They gape at mirrored peaks, reflections of themselves,
> Their treetops bristle at the sight, as though repelled
> By what they see—unforgiving mirrorings of self.

Empedocles of Acragas

I turn away and seek the path of my grand hymn,
To sing of how the world is shaped by Love and Strife
In turns. For Strife and Love were whirling in the vortex
When Strife attained its greatest force and blew apart
The elements that Love once meshed. Every being
Was swept into the gyre, just as dire Charybdis,
Near our Sicilian shores, sucks into its maw each
And every thing, either to regurgitate it back
Again or send it all to hell with no return.
Return is made by way of Love alone, which hovers in
The middle of the vortex, gently chasing Strife till it
Must surface, yielding all to Love. The vortex then
Becomes the Sphere where Kypris Aphrodite rules
And all is peace and harmony. Whatever spins
In Love's embrace is made to mix with other things,
For Strife had meanwhile split apart all that should
Be life and death in one, and all were studying
Some foolish immortality, confused about
Their nature and their destiny, made wise at last
By Love alone. The unmixed now are consummated,
And countless teeming tribes of fertile mortals burst
Gaily forth within the Sphere. They are dispatched
Across the surface of the Earth, the meadows burgeon
With greenery, the seas are full of spawning fish.
Through Love alone the downward plunging curse of Strife
Is lifted. All is recommencement, unchanging change
Is all.

•

You ask me how I know these things, what Muse it was
Enlightened me and banished ignorance and dark
Despair. I will not hesitate to sing the truth,

That you may learn from my own agony and suffering.
O heed the word of this poor fugitive!

•

Far off in Hyperborean lands, remote in the North,
Where ice and winter never seem to cede an inch,
There is another Charybdis. The natives there,
Barbarians with hornèd heads, decked out in furs
Of animals, prefer to call the vortex Maelström.
And in a prior incarnation, long before I was
Both bush and bird, I sailed there in my Sicilian ship,
Well-made, sturdy it was, but not stalwart enough
To save me from the terrors of the Maelström. My ship
Went down for all that mortal man could do and I
Alone survive to tell the tale. The sea there, maddened by
The craggy floor of Tethys and the howling winds above,
A-whirl and churning, sucked me down well-nigh
To Phlegethon and Styx, the rivers of the underworld.
The moon shone full that night, illuminating my
Descent, its light reflecting off the brine as black
As ebony from Africa, now silvered by that moon.
My wounded ship was spinning with alacrity,
So steep the inclination, half the vertical, deadly angle.
I saw below me Chaos itself, a thick mist hovering
Above. The mist itself was covered by a kind
Of rainbow bridge of moon and dewy brine.
The only sign of hope for me was Iris. My ship
Was breaking up, I grasped debris as it stormed by;
Amidst the trash descending down to doom, a narrow
Wooden box collided 'gainst me, the kind of box
Barbarians use to bury their own—a curious custom.
That's when the hymn I sing both now and all my days
First came to me. I seemed to gaze on my pale corpse
Inside the box I gripped, the box of my dear poem
That sings the saving grace, the *Charite* of Love.
My hymn propelled me to the surface of the sea,
Becalmèd now. I was carried to a friendly shore
Where natives gave me shelter, restored my life.

They helped me build a sailing ship, well-equipped,
And I, reborn to life, returned to Sicily my home.
Arrived at Acragas, I was a different creature
Than before, made wise by Maelström and Strife.
My Muse was death itself, which I had met and for
Some little time had left behind. To sing is to
Live on, survival lies in song, to cease is death.

Heraclitus of Ephesus

Should you not have seen the vortex we call Cyclone on the steppes and plains of the broad-breasted Earth, or, most impressively, upon the open seas, you have doubtless seen it on a Hyperborean snow-covered hillside, or, here at Ephesus, over a pile of dead laurel or olive leaves: a kind of joyous circledance at the bottom of the funnel, pure centripetal force pulling all the elements together in a roundelay of pure attraction. In the Cyclone all matter rises, ascending in intensity of pleasure or of pain, ever higher in ever-widening circles, dizzying to those on the outside who merely observe but with ever-greater clarity to those caught up in the pandemonium. Round and round they go, where they stop nobody knows, for there can be no stoppage in the allotment of measured lays, measured not by you or me, make no mistake, but by the Logos. At what must seem the outermost circle of the Cyclone the force is no longer centripetal but suddenly entirely centrifugal; it seems the center itself is swept to the periphery and the periphery knows no bounds. No one can say exactly when attraction becomes repulsion, when centripetal turns centrifugal, but each element in the spin is stretched to the point of annihilation, and the mood is a mix of fascination and panic; all that the whirling element in the grip of the whorl can feel is the power of inevitability that is transporting it from the land of the living to the land of the dead. It is a kind of mortal ecstasy. As the elemental self is dissipating into universal indistinguishable upsurge like a rainbow dewdrop chasing the moon, the disintegrating self is but that alien centrifugal power. Impotently powerful, powerfully impotent. I say it again: mortally immortal, immortally mortal, each living the death of the other and dying its life.

I still can see that beautiful child as she passes. Approach is all. I can feel in her delicate footfall and deliberate gait the outrageous force within her—*in* her, not *of* her. And now I see her hovering on the edge, I see and hear the outrageous centrifugal force, the Cyclonic force that is not her own, surging through her hand and up her slender arm.

Look! Look at her! This child possesses the powerful limb not of a mere mortal but of a god!

The Dagger

The journey of a thousand miles begins with four inches. Allow me to articulate the way stations on that immensely consequential journey.

1. Epidermis, dermis, hypodermis—three layers threaded by an extensive network of nerves across the surface of the body. The loving touch of a hand, when it comes, if it ever does come, begins millimeters above the outermost layer and before all contact, as though the filaments of felt that sprout across the skin had eyes to see what is coming, that gentle touch heralded by some *actio in distans*, and that is how it is with my approach, except that no anticipation can prepare one for the actual onset of puncture and pain. Hence the usual appearance of "hesitation wounds" discovered after the fact, telltale signs of multiple failed attempts. It is important to have no illusions on this point. Pain is the frontier that has to be crossed, and whereas it should be crossed hastily and without hesitation, there is often hesitation. None of us is perfect.

2. Avoid the sternum and do not get lodged between the ribs. Enter anterolaterally on the left between five and four, aiming upward and to the right, do not exceed forty-five degrees, do not look at the breast, do not soften. Do not be disheartened by the fibrous connective tissues beneath the hypodermis, pectoralis major et minor, serratus anterior, subclavius, assorted fascia, which are tough but not tough enough. It is important to have confidence.

3. Pericardium—the sac encasing the heart will fill with blood once the sac wall is breached, thus tamponading the heart and suffocating it, as it were, or better, drowning it in the saline solution that is the inland sea of blood. Yet such tamponading may cause unwanted delay. An adequate sweep of the blade back to the center of the body (see the final step of point 4, below) will speed the process and bring it to successful and timely completion.

4. Epicardium, myocardium, endocardium. Home. The left ventricle, the largest chamber of the heart, unable to hide itself entirely behind the sternum, is exposed and is therefore readily penetrable. Once home, sweep the blade to the right by thrusting the hilt to your left, assuming, as I do,

that you yourself are the operator. Do not, I repeat, do not twist me in the wound, that is merely an expression, a trope, do not be beguiled by a mere figure of speech, do not take it literally, remember the danger of jamming, but sweep the blade to the right, the hilt to the left, as described, if you can, that is, if the heart has not already begun to fibrillate, at which point my work here is done and you fallen senseless.

V

The Nightwatch

Nothing ever happens in this corner of the world; nothing ever transpires in this sleepy Winkel on Rhine. When it does, you can be certain that Hans the village idiot will come on the rip for you, gibbering away and grabbing you by your shirtsleeve just when you've gotten off duty and are ready to turn in for a good day's sleep. He will drag you down to the riverside and lead you a few hundred meters downriver from the village, blathering all the way to Bartholomaeus and the mouth of Magpie Brook.

Constable Schätzle and five or six other men were unfortunately already there when I arrived. Schätzle is a good fellow, a treasure, really. He would make an excellent brother-in-law; he would cause you no trouble. You would not want him as your constable, however.

They had already dragged her half-submerged body by its feet out of the river up onto the bank, and someone was fiddling with her clothing. Another man was about to close her eyelids.

—Please stop whatever you are doing, my friends. Just stop.

I made them tell me what they knew, which was precious little, and I reconstructed the scene. I tried to sift out and discard what they merely surmised although they were absolutely certain of the entire story even if they could not have had the vaguest notion about any of it. The main thing you have to do at a scene is shut your ears to all the drivel and open your eyes to everything in front of you.

—You're looking for clues! cried Hans.

"Clues" is a stupid word. I never use it. What people call a "clue" is what we call *evidence*. And evidence is what it says: it is *evident*. All you have to do is block out the chatter and look, look, look, and keep on looking until you see it. So I looked.

A young woman in white linen slippers and a red dress. Long curling dark hair, tangled now with grass and willow leaves and twigs. Young, early to mid-twenties. A single deep knife wound beneath the left breast. The dress in disarray. But being half-submerged in the river overnight would have done that. Chest uncovered, wound clearly visible. The river did not do those things, neither the one nor the other. It did wash the wound clean. A blue bruise mark bordered the wound, the *meurtrissure*. Above the wound, over the heart, a recent scar, but not from last night.

And the knife? The man who found the body said he had pulled it out and tossed it far out into the Rhine, horrified by what he had stumbled across. But there it was, the knife, just a few feet away, lying in the grass. Who was this man, this confused man who cannot throw to save his life? They told me he was a farmer.

—A farmer? Strange, I thought I knew all the local farmers. All the vintners, too.

—A day laborer, a hireling, they said.

—Ah, an itinerant.

—No, he's been coming here for work every summer for years now. We know him. He's all right. Here he is. His name is Duffre.

Duffre. Strange name. Not from here. The man hung his head. Sheepish. He said not a word.

—Ah, you know him? Good. You can vouch for him.

Silence from the others, silence from Duffre.

I closed my ears even to the silence. Afterward they would all say Duffre was with them in the pub the whole evening swilling beer and they were absolutely certain he'd never left the table which was full of regulars, except to make room for more beer so that he would never have had the time and so on and so forth.

I looked at that red dress. I looked at her shoes. I asked myself who wears a red dress, who wears a long red dress with white linen slippers? and I answered myself not a girl who comes to the river with the intention they told me had brought her to the river, no, a girl who wears a red dress compels her white slippered feet to take her to the river where she plans to meet someone. Perhaps she plans to meet someone who cannot throw to save his life, you never know.

Evidence is what is right in front of you. You merely have to shut your ears and open your eyes.

The wound seemed to have been made from below, not from above, but only the autopsy would determine the angle for certain. An attacker normally would strike from above, but you have to look. I took the length of her. She was tall. If the attacker were a little fellow. . . . I took the length of our day laborer.

Even dullards can read your mind. They saw what I was thinking. They wanted to shut that door, they knew the man, he was a decent chap, a hard worker, it was plainly a suicide, she'd been jilted by her lover, there was a letter. But I always say when you shut a door you cannot see what lies behind it and what lies behind that door could be the evidence you are looking for if you are smart enough to look, and so I never shut a door. Never.

I looked at her arms and hands. Delicate. Thin. I asked myself where is the strength to do the thing they say she has done, the power to drive it home. But I did not see evidence of such strength. I glanced at the knife. I walked over and plucked it out of the grass. I examined it closely. A nasty, silver-studded thing. A dagger, actually. We would have to learn whose it was, would we not? We would preserve it carefully as evidence, the most important piece of evidence, would we not? Safeguarding the evidence is crucial. Put it in the safest possible place, lock it away so it never gets lost.

Her tangled hair was dripping wet. She had fallen onto her back, her upper body going into the river, her feet still on the shore. Her slippers remained dry but for the dew. If she really did do this thing to herself, she must have spun about before falling. If you go to a river to do this thing, then you face the river when you do it. She had to have spun about. Still, with a dagger in your heart, who knows how you spin and fly and fall? You yourself certainly do not know. It's like being caught in a whirlwind.

Schätzle pointed out to me the towel around her neck that I had already seen, a sort of sling. It was filled with a handful of stones, three fist-sized stones. Hardly enough.

—She wanted her body to fall into the river and sink, to cover her shame, observed Schätzle.

—Somebody certainly did want that, I replied.

But either she or her attacker did not succeed. I had to admit that an attacker would have been more proficient at gathering stones and getting rid of the body, unless perhaps he was a man who thought he might also toss the dagger out into the river but then neglected to do that, too. An amateur. An incompetent. A man like any other. A duffer.

Hours passed.

We made the trip downriver to Rüdesheim for the autopsy.

Then back to Winkel and to the church that evening with the coffin in tow for burial the next morning, the July heat already doing what it does.

A surprisingly large crowd for the funeral.

Days passed.

I kept visiting that spot on the Rhine, kept thinking about the scene for many days after the burial, wondering if I had done the right thing. I don't know. But it could well have gone down the way they all had been saying, the Rüdesheim examiner agreeing with them. Still, maybe I should not have given up so soon. Maybe I should have held on to the evidence. I did put it in a safe place.

I sometimes wonder whether I should get into another line of work. Take a day job, sleep nights. Nothing ever happens in sleepy Winkel, but even so.

Before I left the scene I undid and removed the sling. I covered the wound with the upper part of the red dress, the red more intense now than ever, partly because of the river. I closed the eyes. Blue stars.

Father Isinger

I have lost the convert of a lifetime. Whether it would have been my conversion of her or hers of me remained uncertain until today. To win such a soul to Holy Mother Church is the dream of every priest. Yet if she had made a Lutheran of me instead I could have married her and lived a happy life and died a happy death. But it is she—the child—who is dead now, by her own hand, and tomorrow I will lay her to rest here at St. Walburga's.

The bishop will be incensed: a Protestant suicide given a Catholic funeral and buried in sanctified ground? Winkel is a tiny corner of the diocese, however, so that His Grace need never know. My entry into the parish ledger, by this shaky hand, will be cautiously worded, perhaps even disguised. And yet her friends insist on erecting a plaque to her memory, a plaque with a heathen inscription on it, no mention of the Trinity or the Saints. I will place it somewhere down the north wall, near the old crosses, out of sight. Her I will bring to the east wall, as close to my church as possible. Someone is bound to complain. Some cranky parishioner, holier than the Pope, is sure to howl. Even so, the plaque will stand, and I will bury her in the shadow of my church. Let the devil take the hindmost and that howling parishioner too.

We spoke about her death. She felt it coming. Tuberculosis, she said, as with three younger siblings already expired. She seemed so frail, so pale, so defeated. She gave me a little book of her poems. They were odd. She had a strange mind. But she did have a mind—my own a rusted sieve by comparison. One poem I did admire very much, "An Apocalyptic Fragment": *Who has ears to hear, let him hear! a life unending, through all change perdurant!*

In her room at the Zehnthof, her friends the Servière sisters found her bequeathal to St. Walburga's and her written request that she be buried here. She asked that the grave remain hers, that it not be disturbed, that her bones not be exhumed, as though that bit of soil should belong to her forever, as if she wanted to cultivate and enrich that soil for all eternity. She left an offering insufficient for that, but we have the space, I will see to it. She also left a modest bequest to be invested in an account here, with the annual interest to go to the local baker: bread for the school children on every anniversary of her death, the children then to enter the church and pray five Our Fathers and five Hail Marys. Five Hail Marys for a Protestant suicide. *The Lord is with Thee.* I will see to that too.

She told me she had very much wanted to have children.

—But children must have a living mother, she said with a smile.

I had to close my eyes.

The nightwatch and the constable brought the coffin to the church this evening. The thought crossed my mind that I should open it and anoint the body. Baptize her, confirm her, oil her corpse with extreme unction, all in one compact sacramental rite—a rite I was prepared to invent for her. But there had been an autopsy. And everyone had claimed a lock of her hair, a horrid practice I cannot condone. I could not bear the thought of seeing her like that. I did not dare to open it.

All seems lost, but all is not lost. That is what we have to believe.

Achim von Arnim

It has been a month and a day. Poor Günderrode's blue gaze fixes me more unblinkingly now that she can no longer speak. She looks at the whole world with greater freedom now, without holding back. You and I, Bettine, feel more narrowly confined by that gaze. Our own eyes are downcast. We could not give her enough to keep her here, could not sing brightly enough to extinguish the flame of the Furies and rout the doom of that strange passion of hers. I tell you, we—I say "we" and yet I really played no role at all in her life, though I always thought highly of her—I think about that day when in the morning I splashed water in her eyes and in the afternoon she laughed and tried to conceal from me the dagger she had just removed from the closet, and we wrestled over it like children playing with fire until we stumbled against her bed and fell onto it and I held her in my arms, then lifted her up high to heaven. And that evening when I left her standing at her door she looked so lovely—I think of all that and of how we were in awe of her. She was so happy to join in whatever silly games we played back in those carefree, happy times. I think of how timidly she defended herself against Clemens' overbearing schoolmasterly criticisms and censures, so that whenever I think of her now I see a lamb that had nothing more to sacrifice and so sacrificed itself.

But enough of this wretched insanity, this struggle to explain what in itself is entirely clear. Make no claims that go in the direction of good or evil but let all that dissolve like the shadow of a mountain vanishing in the depths of the Rhine. In her final days she wanted to be entirely at one with herself and to find the kind of friendship that heaven alone can grant those on Earth who are lucky enough to be enlivened *together* in all their senses, so that when they die their roots do not strike hard ground but loosen that ground and open it. In this heavenly element of earth even the dagger is turned into a plowshare, the monstrous deed into a bad dream. We have to wipe the tears from our eyes and recognize the deed for what it was, not trying to obliterate it, but trying not to judge it—no one has that right.

Goethe

What causes Ottilie to dwindle and die? She stops eating. She starves the life that was in her. She sees no way out of her situation—no way out but to exit. It is as though the magnetism that is in her and all around her suddenly neutralizes and evaporates, leaving nothing but a trace of regret in the lives of the people who knew her.

Bettine's friend exited quite differently, far more horrifically, perhaps in keeping with her style of writing. Ossian's Darthula—the passionate beauty who sacrifices herself—but to an enemy much closer to home. Unimaginable to me, the deed itself. What could one make of it? What could one say, or write, about it? I take up the pen.

—This Fräulein von Günderrode, who has so recently given us a number of oddly remarkable little poems in dramatic form, has shattered her own form. It seems as though the very ideals expressed in the poems of this young Tian, in company with or wrestling against more earthly passions, have destroyed their otherwise quite admirable vessel.

Yet that says next to nothing; it begs all the questions; it leaves almost everything to speculation and sheer invention. As with Ottilie, she leaves but the barest traces in the lives of others. And what is that—the barest traces? A pile of calcined ash exposed to turbulent weather, to all the whorls of the living.

Bettine's mother took me to the place on the banks of the Rhine near Winkel where Fräulein Günderrode destroyed her body. We stood among the weeping willows there and talked about the catastrophe that had occurred on that very spot some eight years earlier. A pall descended over us, as it always falls over one who stands at the locale where a tragedy has taken place. A moldering log half-sunken in the river, appearing to bend just below the surface, at that moment excited in me no thoughts about refraction; the sudden depth of the water there aroused no profundities but only turbid half-thoughts that soon expired. We were silenced, made mute for some time by the veil that descended over us; the life within us, the life on which we count so desperately, seemed to have drained out of us as well. We were able to extricate ourselves from the feeling of tragedy only by speaking of the sundry ways one has to pursue a life, attain a life, practice a life, preserve the slim advantage of a life against all the odds. It was a banality, of course. But on occasion, dizzied by the whorls of the dead, banality is the only lifeline. The sun set behind us as we walked back to the house.

Friedrich Creuzer

It was all so much trouble when I look back on it. It caused so much confusion, the whole thing. It destroyed my health. My work ground to a halt. She made me detest my Benefactress, she nearly cost me the domestic support and the good order that every man needs. Had it not been for friend Daub I would have been lost forever, submerged in the swamp, drowned in the flood. All that remains now is the cleanup. I must buy up all the fascicles of *Melete*, which has already been printed and is about to be bound—as a noose around my neck. The public dare not see the book, not a single copy dare survive. She made it obvious that her lover Eusebio was I myself, and the publisher Wilmans won't release the entire run to me without payment. Publishers are in it for the money.

Where will I get the funds to buy up all the copies? As always, from the same source. Savigny was born into money, it means nothing to him. And he is a man of the law, which draws money like a magnet. A scholar earns nothing by comparison, even though his studies are so much more demanding. It has always been that way and always will be that way. Savigny knows this, it bites his conscience.

Odd that he was her first lover, I her last. That makes us comrades in arms, I suppose. He wrote me years ago, right after he met her; he wanted to know all about her. Did I know her family? What was she really like? Some said she was timorous to the point of prudishness, others that she was a coquette! Some said she had a vigorously masculine mind, but her blue eyes betrayed pure femininity! Who *was* this heavenly creature? Back then I told him what I knew, which was next to nothing. How things changed!

I sensed that he was jealous when I first told him about us, jealous and no doubt surprised on account of my ugliness. A beautiful man cannot imagine a woman ever falling out of love with him, nor can he imagine an angel falling in love with a hunchback. He never stopped wanting her, although no one ever stops, not even death quells the fire, I could see it in his eyes whenever her name came up in conversation, and he confessed as much to me after he married that dullard Gunda and got mixed up with her absurd family. Whatever could have possessed him? When he could have had the angel and the devil in one, he chose the dullard!

Enough. Savigny too will want all this confusion to die with her. He will want it all to be buried every bit as much as I do. He will not abandon me in my hour of need. After all, we are both victims of Eros, the merciless daemon who strikes rich and poor alike. What chance do we ever have?

Now all I need to do is silence Savigny's absurd in-laws, the yapping brother, the harebrained sister, and his wife, the dullard herself, who is not above the meanest sort of gossip. I will have to enlist all my allies to do that, all my cousins and friends. We will have to reason with the von Heyden woman, quiet the Servière sisters, my god! what a mess Daub made of it! Get those letters back! That is the first thing. Who knows what poison he put into them! If you don't do a thing yourself it doesn't get done right.

Calm yourself. It is all reparable. Restitution of good order there will be. Savigny will help. First things first. Suppress *Melete*. It has no real literary worth. It would have been easy for the poet herself to grant her poems technical perfection, if only she had gone back to them repeatedly and given them form. But that did not seem to be her way. She produced much too much and much too quickly. Care and disciplined attention are always called for when writing—*Melete*, indeed: only a scholar has the training to do these things meticulously. In the end, when my story is told, when I write of my life and work, she will have played no role.

Savigny

I remember her fascination with physiognomy and phrenology. She filled her notebooks with facial types, profiles of the sundry human races, faces of the nations. She drew a splendid portrait of me, which she called "the Frenchman." That made me smile. More striking still was a lovely profile of herself posing as a Circassian of the northern Caucasus. I recognized that bright eye.

No doubt she had fallen under the spell of Lavater, tempted by the extravagant thought that a man's or woman's facial features and shape of head betray their moral character. She was an enthusiast, and not only in this respect: it was a flaw in her character, an error, and I tried to correct it, especially when she fell in love with the wrong man and concocted scheme after scheme to be with him. She carried everything to extremes—the declamatory language of the little dramas she wrote was a symptom of this flaw, a mark of her unreasonable enthusiasms.

As for phrenology, there is something to it, of course. I have seen enough prison inmates to know that much—the beetling brows, the thrusting jaws, the shifty eyes. More revealing than criminals in this respect are our politicians and diplomats. No amount of powder and wiggery can conceal their avarice and artifice and depravity.

It is odd that she attached herself so fervently to Creuzer. She had to overlook a lot of things to do that. Considerable patience and long-suffering there. He with his physiognomy of a criminal—not a violent thug, to be sure, but a coniver, a shrewd confidence man, perhaps even a kind of Iago. Not that I ever really thought of him that way. Back when we were studying at the university we even became friends, and I was able to help him get through the rough patches, and there were a lot of rough patches.

Here we go again.

I will carry out Creuzer's request. I will buy up all the printed sheets of *Melete*. Wilmans will sell them to me, making certain he recovers all his costs, as he should. Creuzer wants me to destroy them all, and I will fulfill his wish—except for one copy. I felt that her second book showed significant improvement over the first. If, as I suspect, this third book of hers shows further progress, I will preserve at least one copy of it. I gave him my word that I would cause the book to disappear, and my word is virtually binding. Yet there are higher laws that govern the preservation of letters and of literature, and no man dare infringe on those laws. I will keep one copy secure—for posterity, as it were. Gunda would not approve, but there is no need to discuss this with her. I will have to make sure it gets into the hands of a reliable colleague, maybe Schlosser. I recall how Karoline responded to Clemens' challenges to her work, especially to his question about her inexplicable need to *publish* her work. I remember her reply well-nigh word for word:

—You wish to know why in the world I had the idea to publish my poems? I have always had the obscure inclination to do so, without asking myself why and wherefore. And now that I have done it I have no regrets, for the longing in me is quite lively and it surges forth again and again—the longing to express my life in durable and worthy form, to join the most excellent ones, to greet them and to be a part of their community. Yes, I have always had a passion for such a community, it is the church toward which my spirit's earthly pilgrimage is perpetually underway.

As for the rest, I will do my best to quiet the women that Creuzer and Daub forced to get mixed up in her death, the von Heyden woman and the Servière sisters. Naturally, the women cannot stop themselves from gossiping. No need to allow them to crucify Creuzer, however. As for Karoline, I cannot silence her, at least not her book, not entirely, lest my mirror cast back at me the physiognomy of a traitor.

Melete

I have straddled the divide between life and death. Why should a human being strive at all in the face of death, I ask myself in such moments. I look forward to every night, preferring unconsciousness and obscure dreams to the brighter life of day, so why should I shudder before the long night and the deep slumber? What deeds await me, or what finer knowledge on the face of the Earth, that I should live any longer?—For a long time I did not know the answer to such questions, which confused me. Then suddenly, in a revelation, everything became clear, and it will remain so eternally. Of course, I know that life is but the product of the most intense attraction and contact of the elements; I know that all its leaves and blossoms, which we call ideas and sensations, must wilt when that contact dissolves; I know that an individual life is given over to the iron law of mortality. Yet as certain as this is to me, another certainty is immured against all doubt—the immortality of life as a whole. For life is precisely this whole, and in the sundry limbs and extremities of this life the elements surge and diminish. And it is also the case that by means of this dissolution (which we sometimes call death) the elements return to the whole that blends them in conformity with the laws of affinity, like to like. Yet these elements alter once they have been compelled upward into life; they become more vigorous, in the way two contestants who have been pitted against each other have grown stronger by the time the contest ends, mightier than they were before. Thus the elements, because they are vital, augment in strength through exercise, as does every vital force.

When the elements return to the earth they enhance the earth's life. But then the earth bears in its womb the stuff of life that has been restored to it and once again gives birth to other appearances of life, until, through ever novel metamorphoses, everything in it that is capable of life has come to life. Such would be the case, at least, if all mass were organic.—

Thus each mortal gives back to the Earth a more elevated and more highly developed elemental life, which the Earth continues to shape into ever ascendant forms. And the organism, absorbing into itself the increasingly developed forms, perforce becomes more perfect and more universal. In this way, the totality comes to be alive precisely through the downfall of particularity, and particularity lives on deathlessly in the totality whose life it has vitally augmented, such that after its death the particular itself is elevated and multiplied, and so through both living and dying helps actualize the Idea of the Earth. Thus, however my elements may be scattered, whenever they are gathered up into something that is alive they will elevate it, and if gathered into something whose life is very like a death they will nonetheless ensoul it.—

Whether the Earth will succeed in organizing itself to immortality I do not know. It may be that a faulty ratio of essence to form remains in its primal elements, and this will hinder that organization. Perhaps the totality of our solar system will be required to achieve such an equilibrium. Perhaps this too, in turn, will not suffice, and it will be a task for the entire universe.

That blessed universal state, however, becomes increasingly remote with every act of deception, injustice, and selfishness, whereby the god of Earth is manacled in newly forged chains. The longing of that god for a better life expresses itself in our own innermost core as our receptivity to excellence. In the wounded conscience, however, such longing must lament the fact that its blessedly divine life lies afar, off in the remote.

Bonaventura

I love this callisthenic view of life, which believes that exercise makes us stronger—truly, I do love it. Yet at some point the fibers deteriorate and calisthenics must confess its diminished efficacy. I wonder if the elements retain their identity while expanding their horizons, if they grow wider and deeper and stronger, or if they merely do whatever they can do and then shrivel. Are not gestation, birth, and childhood the periods of miracle, when vitality is highest? Is not all the rest decline and fall? See how the children in their earliest months master the world—if they survive—and come to speak whatever languages they hear as soon as they hear them. And see how, grown old, they become too brittle for the world and too demented for the word. In the end they cannot even speak the one language they have spoken over a lifetime. No, the elements do enhance themselves through use and stress and toil but only up to the point where they can no longer carry the burden assigned them. The turning point, the apogee, initiates the greater mystery, and it takes a greater faith to understand the way down and to affirm it. To believe that perigee does not follow apogee is sheer hopefulness, and that is a form of stupor, and stupor a sign of incipient collapse.

I love the fertilizer theory of life as well. Plant a dead fish alongside each grain of corn and you will have bread. But first you need a dead fish, and that is a fish that has met and passed its turning point. Without mortality, immortality starves. Perhaps it is merely a question of point of view. But do inquire of the dead fish if you desire to learn the more trustworthy view. Perhaps the way down is the way up, but it is less fishy to think that the way up is the way down. Quite a ways down.

If all mass were organic, then life would seem always to ascend. Must whatever rises converge? I wonder if it does not rise simply to fall. Gravity is not for nil. If wishes were horses, beggars would spare the soles of their shoes. But saving soles is the craft of cobblers, not of preachers and deceivers. I hear the latter prattling on as I listen in nocturnal doorways and at fogged windowpanes.

I admire too the balloon idea of Earth, what a lark, ever ascending, up, up, up, in the air. But to be up in the air is to be stumped. And love, the heated gas that bears our balloon upward, will invariably reach the point of combustion, we will feel ourselves flailing and failing and falling, and that will have been the turning point, the onset of perigee, of nadir. Young Icarus too once loved.

Achim von Arnim

I am uncertain whether a writer ever really understands what she or he is writing—even after the work is done. I thumbed through one of my early pieces, the "Melück" story, which I called "an anecdote." But it is at least two anecdotes capped by a terribly jarring third anecdote that has nothing to do with the first two. Or everything to do with them—I cannot figure it. The third anecdote is jarring in any case, perhaps because it betrays the hidden story behind the first two.

It must have been five years or so after Karoline's death. Every detail of that death shattered me. I remember being especially outraged by the local constable's insistence that an autopsy be performed. That poor delicate body had suffered cutting enough. But I knew why he insisted on it. He was hoping to find evidence of a mortal disease; if they could prove that her death was already at work in her, then it would not have been suicide, and she could be granted a Christian burial. The pathologist dutifully found "irregularities" in the marrow of her spine; he declared that she was splenetic, hypochondriac, and heaven knows what else. Finally, he announced his incredulity that such a delicate creature could ever have found the strength to drive the dagger home, as though such a man could ever in his life comprehend the strength of the spirit in her. Even if the excellent doctor lived to be a hundred he would never understand the violence she called upon to escape the life that was oppressing her; he would never possess the life force that would enable him to comprehend the heart of hearts in that incomparable woman, abandoned, utterly alone in that moment, emptied of hope.

The anecdote—or the three anecdotes compressed into one—to which I gave the title "Melück Maria Blainville: the Local Prophetess of Arabia" was a love story, a story of "frightful love," as I called it. A girl banished from her homeland sails westward from the port at Smyrna to Toulon, where a French family adopts her. She seems to unite the best qualities of both sexes, we are told, and that alone should have alerted me to the person I was writing about. She leaves the cloister to which she has been sent (the "Residence"?) before they can make a nun of her, and she becomes an actress in the theater at Marseille. A young count, heretofore devoted to a woman of high repute and unsullied character, Mathilde by name, loses his heart to Melück. Literally, as we soon learn. For Melück turns out to be a witch rather than a mere prophetess. She enchants the count and steals his heart. She absconds with the principal organ of his life, even though the count does not notice that he has been so deprived. He can survive from now on only in the closest proximity to her, that is, by sleeping in her bed. *His gentle heart melted in Melück's hands like a costly balm; it all led to pleasure, and Melück denied him nothing.*

The count trusts that there are two kinds of love, one heavenly and one profane; as long as his virginal Mathilde remains ignorant of the affair, he may enjoy both loves. Yet Mathilde does not remain ignorant. Crisis. Because the count has lost his heart to Melück, however, Mathilde understands that the three of them must live together. They must dream the dream of a heaven on earth. End of the first anecdote.

Already at this point I ask myself the question: Who here, in *this* story, is Karoline? Surely, she is the pallid Mathilde, not the dusky Melück. Certainly, to love Karoline would not be *to fall into the hands of a heart-devouring magician.* And yet. What if you have fallen in love with your wife's best friend? What if you fell in love with her on some rainy afternoon long ago, so long ago and so hopelessly that the death of your wife's friend only aggravates the betrayal, setting a mortal seal on it forever? Would that not be a proof of witchery, or at least of sorcery?

Melück is Persephone. She eats the seed of a pomegranate and thus becomes the queen of the dead. Did I love the queen of the dead? Did she indeed gnaw at the purloined heart of me? Had she absconded with the very core of me?

—He will not get his heart back, proclaims Melück. He must stay with me, because his heart is in me. . . . I want nothing else from him than his constant closeness. His wife may be happy with his existence in the cosmos. His heart is in me, without me he cannot live, and he will live only as long as I live.

Melück grants Bettine—sorry, Mathilde—the cosmos. Me she will have up close, inside her body.

The second anecdote recounts the familiar fact that the French Revolution begins with high ideals but soon becomes the Terror. The local rabble sack the count's castle. The leader of the rabble, who has always lusted after the prophetess, stabs Melück in the back, presumably through the heart. She and the count fall dead at the same instant, since she has long possessed *his* heart. Mathilde and her children survive and escape the mob, *as though leaving Sodom behind them*, but Mathilde notices for the first time that her children have *eyes that come out of the East and have very long eyelashes*, Melück's lashes, Karoline's lashes. End of second anecdote.

Our children too, Bettine's and mine, are they in fact Karoline's babies? Has she somehow taken them from us by absconding with my heart?

The third anecdote, the terrible and terrifying anecdote, begins with a sudden shift of scene: an unexplained leap from Mediterranean France to the Rhine River near Winkel, *the shores where we lived*, as the story confusedly says, since no character in either anecdote has ever lived there. The narrator's boat or raft is tied to *a half-submerged willow tree*. Whereupon, the following scene ensues, the baffling dénouement of the tale, as though it had anything to do with the stories of Melück of Araby or the French Revolution. For this is the scene involving those who mourn Karoline's demise.

—We disembarked and looked at one another silently, pointing to the tongue of land that gradually sank into the stream. A noble life, holy to the Muses, sank into guiltless madness there, and the stream erased the sacred spot and bore it away so that it could never be desecrated. O wretched songstress, can the Germans of our time do nothing more than silence the lovely one, silence her to death, consign that exemplary person to oblivion, thus committing a sacrilege against everything that ought to be taken in earnest? Where are your friends? No one has gathered up for posterity the traces of your life and your inspiration; fear in the face of the sort of people who will never lift a finger for the sake of the good has crippled them all. Now for the first time I understand the writing on the wall at your gravesite, the letters now almost entirely eroded by heaven's tears; now I know why you cite there all the elements that pertain to you, but why you make no mention at all of human beings!—And, deeply moved, we dwell on the inscription as one of us recites it to the others who have forgotten it:

Earth, you my mother, and you my nurturer, breath of air, holy Fire, friend to me, and you O my brother, mountain stream, and my father, the Aither, I give you all friendly thanks and pay you my respects; I have lived with you here below and I go to the other world, happy to be leaving you. Farewell, then, brother and friend, father and mother, farewell!

Bettine

Oh, my memory of her has become a pale shade, and this enrages me! Like the others, I too could not hold onto this love of mine! I am not good, I am not strong, I cannot paint a firm memory within me of the one who was always good to me; some novel distraction always diverts me, so how can I promise to remember anything at all? I am weak. It would be far better if I were more serious, less rash.—O God, help me to bear this burden that I am, let me make all those who demand something of me happy, but give me also the energy, courage, and insight to do and to be that, help me not to be unjust. If you should give me the strength for a new love, then grant me double the strength for the old; let me be a sacrificial victim of that old love, let me be just, let me be a delight to others and to myself—but that would be to grant me heaven on earth! How can I pray so blasphemously?

And yet I do pray. Suddenly I am transported once again to that terrible shore. The early morning fog is rising off the Rhine. We beach our raft and huddle together beneath the willows on the sandy bank. Her pale shade is touched now by Eos the dawn, it takes on color and form, becomes flesh. Yes! I have her now! I have her now and always!

You ask me whether after all these years I still remember what she looked like, whether she appears to me now in dreams and visitations. I reply that I need no dreams or apparitions. She is with me every day and every night of my life, I need only look. There she is. There she stands. Ask away.

—Her hair. What was her hair like?

—Glistening. Dark brown to black, in the sun jet black. Sometimes she wore it bound up in a nest of curls. Usually she let the curls loop and plunge as they would, draping over her shoulders and down her back.

—And her eyes?

—Sappho says that when the moon is at the full, the stars, awestruck, recede and vanish from the sky. She had lunar eyes, the owl eyes of Pallas Athena, pale blue in color, a kind of gray-blue, like the color of the sky after sunset. Eyes like blue flames whenever an idea took hold of her, or like the blue of the sea, silver in the noonday sun, the sea where you wanted nothing more than to bathe naked in its swell.

—Her brow? What was her forehead like?

—Smooth and white as ivory. Like a cathedral arch, free and open, though not as lofty as all that. Not a high brow, but wide, expansive, like Plato's brow. Sometimes I gave her that name. Plato the wrestler. Günter! And eyelashes that curled up toward that brow with a smile. Eyebrows sometimes like two glowering dragons taking my measure as she gazed, not seizing me but not releasing me either, her hackles rising to frighten me when my idleness irked her. But then the dragons would relent, almost anxiously. That's the way each eyebrow observed you, alert to resist your blandishments and attack you when that was needed and yet made timid by even the most gentle remonstrance.

—And her nose? her cheeks? Tell us everything.

—Somewhat proud, that nose, expressing something like contempt, some said, but that was because of the dilation of the nostrils, since she could scarcely control her breathing when thoughts ascended from her lower lip, which pursed strongly—Oh, for a kiss from that lip!—although supervised and restrained by that refined upper lip. And her chin, I have to tell you about that! For, truly, I have not forgotten that Erodion, the God who is Eros, as you may say, enthroned himself there. He left a mark there with his finger, a slight cleft in the chin, a kind of spiritual fold that I would enter with my eyes when she recited her poems to me, when all their splendid wisdom whelmed me!

—What is she holding in her hand?

—I cannot make it out. But you do not ask me the important questions. You do not ask me what it was to love such a woman and to be loved by her. You do not ask me what it means to have lost such a woman. And it is good that you do not ask me these things.

I read my book again and I search for the answers. My book breathes not a word about her death and my own desolation. Not a word about my self-sealing oblivion. How could it? My book has no eyes to see. Whatever insight may be in it flows from her, and I need her here now to give me the answers.

My friends and I hover on the riverbank near Bartholomaeus. She haunts the place, silent but for the quiet wash of Magpie Brook into the Rhine. My dear husband remembers the plaque on the churchyard wall at St. Walburga's and he recites the final echoes of her—echoes of earth, air, fire, water.

sappho

i have a golden daughter lovely as a flower. to me you once did seem a small ungainly girl, but i would not trade you for all the gold in lydia. stand up and look into my face, sweet love, unleash on me the awful beauty of your eyes. eventide, return to me what the light of day bedazzled, bring home the lamb, bring home the kid, bring home the child to its mother.

and now the night. the stars around the radiant moon will fade and hide their glittering sparkle when she is at the full and shines upon the earth and all the world goes silver. now comes the midnight hour, and soon enough midnight is gone, the moon is down, δέδυκε μενὰ σελάννα, the pleiades pass, the hours fly, you lie alone.

i hear your lamentation *oh my girlhood has left me, oh my early years where have you gone* and the brazen reply *nevermore, no, nevermore shall i return to you* and you with forceful voice *then shall i remain unwed for all eternity!* ἀϊπάρθενος ἔσσομαι.

you wrap yourself in gossamer garments, a broidered strap of exquisite lydian work covers your feet. i place a cushion beneath your head. no girl more wise than you will ever see the sun. come to her now, dark-eyed hypnos, come to the child of night, that she may sleep in the bosom of the one she loves. this is all the dust she leaves behind, for she has passed before her wedding day to the darkling chamber of persephone. atop the tree, at the farthest end of its uppermost bough, ripens the most perfect apple, not overlooked by the harvesters but well beyond their reach, for so it is with all the best things. and now her friends will take a razor to their hair and shear it off in grief, all those lovely tresses on the ground, but you my dear must wreathe sweet garlands through your hair and with your slender hands weave shoots of dillweed for your diadem, for the graces grace those who wear blossoms in their hair and spurn the ungarlanded. a sweet look alights now on her fair face. i think that even in years to come people may remember us.

Clemens Brentano

I should not have written to her about blood. It was not about sucking blood. That was not the liquid I meant. Well, then, what? After these dead children of mine, and after the daunting Mereau too has hemorrhaged to her death, her death and her last infant's death and my own death in one final gushing—I saw the drenched midwife after it was over, she tried to hide herself from me—what now? And why am I dwelling on *her* after all these years, she who never let me get near her, the long-legged timorous forbidding goddess—those eyes! I cannot close them!

No, it was not about blood. That was synecdoche. It was about the milk she never gave me, the milk Mereau allowed me with each pregnancy, there was an overabundance of milk, daunting she was but not ungenerous. It was about the sap she never accepted from my tremulous tree, I who would have surrendered it all to her, all my sap and all my lymph and plasma, all of it, to her. Through all her feints and evasions I could feel the smoldering heat in her; not a raging fire, not a conflagration, smokeless embers only, but fire nonetheless. She burned for me even as I disgusted her. She was ardent for me, her naughty boy, even though it was our good Savigny she truly wanted, or the dwarfish and desiccated Creuzer. Or perhaps yet another. Perhaps my own brother-in-law, that other boy with the magic horn, beautiful Achim. That may well be. Yet still I think she burned for me.

I felt it especially at Trages, where they made us sleep separately in the outlying buildings that were farthest apart from each other. A tribe of chaperones surrounded us, ruining every chance to meet alone. Our friends could sense the love force rising in me, no doubt, but they felt it stirring in her as well. It was to protect Bettine that they kept us apart, I do not doubt it, since my dear sister would have been crushed by jealousy. Bettine too felt that fire in the goddess she worshiped, she sensed it as much as I did, but I know she did not get any closer to the hearth than I did.

All that milk and all that furious blood gone now to powdery ash. All that future gone to bootless irrecoverable past. And the ocean she bore inside her—dried up by now, a dead sea, a desert. Why dwell on her now? After all these beloved defunct of my own, all these catastrophes of mating and birthing and dying, why dwell at all on the child who disappointed me most?

Her friends warned her not to trust me, said I was a leaky vessel. They were right, of course. But I wrote her and confessed everything.

—You have a sterling heart, you know how to forgive, and I feel that I need your forgiveness if I am ever to achieve the tranquility I need but probably will never find. I go begging at every door for alms of forgiveness. No heart has ever suffered the storms my heart has suffered, raging tempests and silent squalls, the rocky cliffs themselves should weep. O gaze on the flowers of spring and let them be the children who plead my cause. O let the nightingale touch your heart with songs of reconciliation. And so farewell, my child, whether man or woman or whatever else you may have been, you are my beloved, follow me, for how can I trace you now? If you wish to turn your back on me and crush me, my gaze will follow you still, will go to meet you—intuiting, weeping, espying, glimpsing you again in pleasure and in pain, prayerfully in pious love, you swimming across the night sky or rooting yourself meditatively in the grave—the gaze is ever an affair of the eye, until the eye breaks and becomes what it once was: light.

And you now? Where are you, lovely child of my youth, where are you now that all around us silence reigns and the moon, mournful and splendid, rises over mountain peaks? Where are you now if not in this unending poem I shall call *Night*?

> Dead silence surrounds me this night, and thirst and love and dying!
> A taciturn sky nocturnal over my head, the holy face is veiled. . . .
> > Sleep sweetly, you, my lovely child!
> See, beside your cradle, the bloom I place there, the blossoming rose,
> The radiant rose that, keeping still, tells everyone what no one knows.

The Dagger

It is dark in here, dark and dank and cold. I am narrowly confined. I do not know where I am.

I weary of being blamed for her death. She did not need me for that. She took everything, not only me, to heart. Least of all did she need me for the wounding. She had people to do that work. Or, it may be, her heart was a self-inflicted wound.

Centuries have passed, it seems, centuries like days to me. I exist still—and stilly—somewhere. I am uncertain where. I am vague about so many things. I have lost a bit of my edge. If our appetites are not whetted from time to time we grow dull, we lose the point of our existence. I dream sometimes of ancient battles, campaigns, sieges, unholy massacres. I sense that they are going on all around me still, but I play no part in them. Now and then the earth trembles. Quake? Cannonfire? Bombardment? I cannot tell. I am left to riddle on the continuities.

I overheard the men that day on the banks, the men who said I had been tossed into the river. They claimed that boatmen on the river had seen me darting across the night sky like a comet and had heard the splash, but they were saying this at the moment those inquisitive fingers lifted me out of the grass. I was not dripping, unless with dew, but he handled me cautiously. I felt his prying eye on me. He wanted to question me closely. I remained discreet.

After every engagement, I withdraw somewhat. I grow less communicative than I otherwise would like to be. Battle-weary? No, I don't think so. Self-absorbed, inward-turning, reflective, perhaps. Thinking, perhaps, as I lay there in the grass while the men were speculating and that canny hand retrieved me, thinking that in the end I had begun to grow fond of her in spite of myself. She was inordinately proud of me. She showed me to her friends; her friends recoiled in horror. It was wonderful. That otherwise unfamiliar smile on her face, a look almost haughty, that glint in the eye!

It was different when we slept together. There were no smiles then. She held me close. That was an awkward engagement for me, I was unprepared for it, but over the years we were together I gradually succumbed to it—that unaccustomed warmth. And I gradually accepted that her need of me was fundamentally different from anything I had ever known.

Over the centuries I have become increasingly neutral in questions of religion. Slaughtering Christians, an activity in which I once fervently believed, even relished, now seems to me quaint. Yet her elevating me to the status of Redeemer seems equally absurd. Even so, there was the warmth, the warmth of her bedclothes and her body.

Perhaps I did succumb. But I prefer to think of us as companions in arms, as in one of her stories. Two going together. Hand in gauntlet.

Sometimes a memory is so vague, so blurred and indistinct, you have no way of knowing whether it is a true memory or an airy fancy. But that canny man who picked me up at the riverbank and eyed me so perspicuously—did he, late that same day, when all was done, against his own better judgment, slip me into the coffin before it was nailed, sealed, and sent to the priest? That would be some comfort to me.

Acknowledgments

I am grateful to Dagmar von Gersdorff for her excellent biography, *Die Erde ist mir Heimat nicht geworden: Das Leben der Karoline von Günderrode* (Insel Verlag, 2006), which was a mainstay for the project; to Birgit Weißenborn, who edited Günderrode's correspondence, *"Ich sende Dir ein zärtliches Pfand": Die Briefe der Karoline von Günderrode* (Insel Verlag, 1992); to Ute Weinmann, *Karoline von Günderrode: Eine Annäherung an die Lebensgeschichte der Dichterin und an ihre Spuren in Winkel ab 1806* (Reichert Verlag, 2023); also helpful, especially for Günderrode's debt to Schelling's philosophy, is Markus Hille, *Karoline von Günderrode* (Rowohlt Taschenbuch Verlag, 1999); essential now is the three-volume historical-critical edition of her work, *Karoline von Günderrode Sämtliche Werke und Ausgewählte Studien*, edited by Walter Morgenthaler (Stroemfeld/Roter Stern, 2006). There is growing interest in her work in the English-speaking world. See, for example, Anna C. Ezekiel, *Karoline von Günderrode: Poetic Fragments* (State University Press of New York [SUNY series in Contemporary Continental Philosophy], 2016), and Joanna Raisbeck, *Karoline von Günderrode: Philosophical Romantic* (Legenda, 2022).

My thanks to Helmbrecht Breinig and Susanne Opfermann, who first awakened my interest in Günderrode and took me to the Savigny estate at Trages; to Iliana Tsoukala of Freiburg University, who gathered all of Günderrode's correspondence for me; to the helpful staff at Das Freie Deutsche Hochstift in Frankfurt, and especially to Prof. Dr. Wolfgang Bunzel, Dr. Konrad Heumann, and Dr. Katja Kaluga; to Frau Angela Baronin von Brentano at the Brentanohaus, Winkel-am-Rhein, who supplied much information about Winkel, the Brentano family, and Günderrode herself.

My thanks also to Gabriel Meyer of the Heidelberg University Archive, who clarified matters concerning the image that serves as the frontispiece to this book, and to Elisabeth Honerla of the Insel Verlag for explaining to me that the image is in the public domain. According to Dagmar von Gersdorff (*Die Erde ist mir Heimat nicht geworden*, 28–29 and 220), the so-called "Heidelberg Miniature" was a cameo sent by Karoline von Günderrode to Friedrich Creuzer, who valued it highly as a likeness of Günderrode herself; yet the image, as Gabriel Meyer informed me, is actually based quite closely on an engraving by Francesco Bartolozzi (1728–1815) with the title "La Sainte Vierge." Bartolozzi's engraving appears in the collections of the Herzog Anton Ulrich-Museum in Braunschweig and in the Albertina of Vienna. It is therefore impossible to say whether the cameo image is a true likeness of Günderrode or not. Why then have I reproduced it here? Because the only extant portrait we have of Günderrode, widely available in the literature, was said—by Karoline's sister Charlotte—to bear no resemblance at all to Karoline herself. Whether Bartolozzi's engraving comes closer remains a mystery.

With regard to the three remaining illustrations, all from Günderrode's notebooks, I thank the Universitätsbibliothek Johann Christian Senckenberg Frankfurt am Main for their generous permission to reproduce them here; the aid of the library's Raschida Mansour and the Freies Deutsches Hochstift's Esther Woldemariam and Wolfgang Bunzel were indispensable in this regard, and I am grateful to them.

My thanks, further, to Alexander Bilda of Freiburg University, who helped with the research; to Ulrich Halfmann, Helmbrecht Breinig, Walter Brogan, Charles Scott, and Nancy Tuana for reading earlier drafts of the book; to the three very generous and helpful reviewers of the manuscript for SUNY Press and to Dr. Michael Rinella and the entire staff at SUNY Press, especially Rebecca Colesworthy, Jenn Bennett-Genthner, Susan Kauffman, Kate Seburyamo, and Michelle Alamillo; to Dennis J. Schmidt, the series editor, for his unwavering support; to Joe Kemming, my co-worker, neighbor, and friend, who took me to Winkel and grieved with me there; to Amane Kaneko and David Matthew Krell, who designed the cover; to Lisa Rone, who gave me the idea of suicide as a vortex, maelstrom, or cyclone that sweeps away the psyche; and to Nancy Tuana and Charles Scott once again for the white slippers.